Secrets

OF

Willow Springs

Book 2

The Amish of Lawrence County Series

Tracy Fredrychowski

ISBN 978-1-7342411-0-5 (paperback)
ISBN 978-1-7342411-1-2 (digital)

All Bible verses taken from New Life Version Bible (NLV) and the New King James Version (NKJV)

Published in South Carolina by The Tracer Group, LLC
https://tracyfredrychowski.com

Contents

A Note about Amish Vocabulary

The language the Amish speak is called Pennsylvania Dutch and is usually spoken rather than written. The spelling of commonly used words varies from community to community throughout the United States and Canada. Even as I did research for this book, the spelling of some words changed within the same Amish community that inspired this story. In one case, spellings were debated between family members. Some of the words may have slightly different spellings, but all come from the interactions I've had with the people in the Amish settlement near where I was raised in northwestern Pennsylvania.

While this book was modeled upon a small Amish community in Lawrence County, this is a work of fiction. The names and characters are products of my imagination and do not resemble any person, living or dead, or actual events that took place in that community.

List of Characters

Emma Byler. (aka Elizabeth Cooper) A kind and thoughtful sixteen-year-old Amish girl who feels *Gott* is calling her to help her birth mother find her way back to her faith. Leaving her Amish family in Willow Springs to go to Sugarcreek only adds to the tension in the Byler family.

Daniel Miller. The twenty-one-year-old English brother to Emma. After encouragement from his adoptive father, Daniel takes Elizabeth to Sugarcreek to meet her mother. As the only living male in his family, does he have what it takes to hold his family together?

Marie Cooper. The forty-year-old biological mother to Daniel and Elizabeth. After spending the last sixteen years in prison, can Marie find a way to be accepted in the town she once called home and by the children she didn't get a chance to raise?

Nathan Bouteright. After losing his *fraa* in an accident, Nathan is forced to hire an English woman to care for his *kinner* and his ailing *Mamm*.

Rosie Bouteright. When arthritis prevents Rosie from caring for Nathan's *kinner,* she helps the only way she knows how – by recognizing *Gott*'s plans.

Sarah Mast. More than once, Sarah has upset Nathan to the point that he realizes he might be confusing his feelings for his late *fraa* with his sister-in-law, Sarah.

Matthew Byler. Emma's twenty-two-year-old *bruder*, Matthew, encourages her to follow her heart and explore her *Rumspringa* without the approval of Jacob.

Jacob & Stella Byler. The Amish parents of Emma.

Rebecca & Anna Byler. Emma's eighteen-year-old twin *schwesters*.

Samuel Yoder. Giving Emma the space she needs to handle the drama being forced on her, Samuel takes a back seat to his own desires and waits for her in Willow Springs.

Katie Yoder. Samuel's younger *schwester* and Emma's best friend.

Anna Mae Troyer. Jacob Byler's sixty-year-old *schwester* from Sugarcreek.

Bishop Melvin Shetler. A leader in his Sugarcreek *g'may*, Bishop Shetler is forced to come to terms with the choices he's made.

Lilian Shetler. Wife to Melvin Shetler.

Prologue

August 2017 - Sugarcreek, Ohio

The early morning light had just started to flood the corridor when the seven o'clock bell rang. The steel lock that kept Marie Cooper in her cell slid open, and an armed guard was waiting to escort her to Processing. Pushing herself off the bottom bunk, she reached for the small canvas bag at her feet that contained her meager belongings and headed for the door. Stopping only for a second to look back and wave goodbye to her cellmates, she suddenly felt a sense of sadness. These women had become like family. Even though she hated to admit it, she felt closer to them than she did her own.

Walking through the double doors that separated her from the outside world, Marie was stopped and patted down by two female guards. Once through the reception area, she found herself sitting at a desk listening to the monotone voice of the discharge officer. Signing her name to a form indicating she understood she could not vote, carry a firearm or leave the state of Ohio, she then laid the pen aside and folded her hands on her lap. Her heart raced as the officer read the date and time she was to report to her probation officer and the monthly amount that would be due in thirty days to pay her fines.

After the officer finished all of her release documents, she directed Marie to move to the counter at the back of the room. There she found herself looking down at the items that had been emptied out in front of her. Listening to the inventory being rattled off by the large woman behind the counter, each piece forced her to remember something she had tried hard to forget.

"One gold band."

Against the wishes of her mother, Marie had run away with the first boy who paid any attention to her. When the bruises became too hard to conceal, and all of her mother's predictions came true, she cut off all ties with her.

"One pair of jeans and one pink T-shirt."

The blue stretchy material reminded her that she hadn't even gotten a chance to work off her pregnancy weight before being arrested.

"One nursing bra."

Just another reminder that she never got to raise her daughter. The sound of a baby crying still haunted her dreams.

"One necklace."

At the age of fourteen, after giving her life to Christ, her mother surprised her with the simple gold cross. It was all she had to remember her by now.

The woman pushed another form at her to sign and pointed to the area where she could change out of her prison clothes and into the ones in front of her. She scooped up her belongings and headed to the changing room.

Closing the door with her foot, she leaned back and tried to ward off the tears that were pooling in her eyes. This day was supposed to be happy, but the fear she felt was traumatizing.

Pulling the prison issued blue shirt over her head, she caught a glimpse of herself in the mirror. Her golden hair was now showing signs of silver flecks at her temples, and the brown eyes that once had been full of hope and wonder had turned cold and lifeless.

Slipping her legs into the loose jeans, she realized not only had her body changed, everything about her was different. Years in prison had hardened her, and she wasn't sure she liked who she saw in the mirror.

She had failed her children, but more importantly, she felt like she had failed God. Killing her husband to protect an Amish man she didn't know, giving her baby away to a stranger and signing over her parental rights so her son could be adopted had changed her. The only stability in life had been her mother, and she had long passed away. She had no one who cared or, better yet, no one who loved her. Daniel Miller, her son, was only helping her out of duty, and he'd made it clear he wasn't happy about letting her back into his life. He was her only connection to the outside world she had been shut off from for so long.

After pushing the gold band in her pocket, she clasped the necklace around her neck and laid her hand over the cross that fell in the hollow of her neck. At one time the cross meant the world to her, but years of feeling abandoned by God left her full of resentment. No matter how she looked at it or how many prison ministers had tried to reach out to her, she couldn't let go of the feeling of being forgotten by God.

A hard knock on the door reminded her that she was still under the watchful eye of the guard. She was taking too much time changing her clothes.

Opening the door, she walked past the guard and handed the woman at the desk her neatly folded pile of prison clothes. After the guard asked her a series of questions about who was picking her up and if she understood she had an appointment with her parole officer the next day, she was instructed to sit in the reception area to wait for her ten o'clock release time.

The hands on the clock above the door made a loud click as it reached nine. Again, the fear she was fighting started to take over.

What will happen if Daniel doesn't come pick me up? Where will I go? How will I get to my appointment tomorrow?

Her stomach churned as she tapped her fingers on the wooden arms of the chair. That voice, there it was again.

She closed her eyes and tried to get it to leave. It was getting louder and louder. No matter how hard she tried to push the words away, the whispers kept coming. Deep down she knew who it was, but she wasn't ready to listen. Like a voice a million miles away she heard. *"Do not be terrified, do not be discouraged, for the Lord your God will be with you wherever you go."*

She shook her head, trying to quiet the small voice. *Where have I heard that before? Was it one of the Bible verses Mother often read to me or was it a Sunday school memory verse playing in my head?*

Wherever it was, she knew she needed to put her trust in God. But years of torment left her feeling that she could count on only one person, herself.

Picking up the bag at her feet, she peered inside making sure she had everything with her. *Is this all I have to show for thirty-nine years?*

She pulled the ring from her pocket and put it in the bag as she picked up the torn and tattered picture of a baby. There was no way for her to know what Elizabeth looked like or even how she'd spent the first sixteen years of her life. The unanswered letters she'd sent to the address where she'd left her gave her no hope. She begged Daniel to visit the address in Sugarcreek to see if he could find his sister, but she had not heard if he had gone.

Aside from the picture, she had a few short letters from Daniel that were anything but short and to the point. She owned a brush, a toothbrush and a picture of her mother. What fond memories she had of her mother. It didn't matter that her father had died when she was five, her mother worked hard to support them and always made it a priority to raise her in a good Christian home.

How was she ever going to face it all without her mother by her side? She felt all alone in a world that had shown her no mercy. Harshly sentenced for a crime by a judge who was out to use her as an example and married to a man who used her as a punching bag, life as she saw it was hopeless.

The room was cold and lifeless, just like her cell had been, and Marie was anxious to leave the bitterness behind. How was she ever going to ward off these dark feelings? Sitting on the stand beside her was a leather-bound Bible. Instantly her hand was drawn to it. Instead of opening it, she laid her hand on top of it. Memories of the well-worn pages of her mother's Bible flashed in her head. A warm feeling passed through her hand. She jerked it away as if she'd touched something hot.

"Cooper."

Startled by the buzz that unlocked the door, Marie needed a minute to realize her name had been called. She watched the door swing open.

8

Standing on wobbly legs, she passed the guard seated at the entrance. Without looking up, he instructed her that her ride was waiting in the parking lot near the front security checkpoint.

Stepping outside she closed her eyes and raised her face to the sun. It felt warmer, the air fresher than it had ever felt before. A dragonfly fluttered in front of her nose and made her smile. The first real genuine smile she'd had in years. For a moment, chills ran down her arms, and warmth surrounded her like someone had embraced her in a loving hug. One single tear rolled down her cheek as she pushed the feeling away. Marie shook her head back to reality.

Focusing her eyes toward the security gate, she saw a man, not the boy she'd left behind. Daniel was leaning up against his truck, his arms folded tightly across his chest. Her heart ached to hold him close and tell him how sorry she was. He'd been through so much because of the choices she'd made. How was she ever going to mend his broken heart?

Chapter 1 – Emma's Parents

July 17th, 2017 - Willow Springs, PA

Daniel stopped the truck as soon as he turned into Emma's Amish parents' driveway and looked over at his sister. Emma sat with her head down, wringing the tissue she held in her hands. Her tears had long dried, but the after-effect of the day's events still showed on her face. He watched as she looked out the passenger window over toward the Byler's Handmade Furniture sign. Nodding her head, she took a deep breath in and let it out in a deep sigh, trying to brace herself to see her parents.

Daniel put the truck in Park and said. "We can sit here for as long as you want."

Not wanting to rush her, he sat and let the silence between them calm her.

"It was just a few days ago you helped me plant those flowers, and we talked about you going to Sugarcreek to find your sister," Emma finally said, still looking at her *datt's* sign. "One minute I wished you luck, and the next I find out I'm her. I don't feel like your sister, Elizabeth Cooper."

Daniel just let her talk. He didn't need to add to her confusion. At this point, he didn't know how to help. He was in as much shock as she was. The sister he had been searching for was right under his nose all along. They both had a lot to think about, and most of all, they had to come to terms with the notion that their biological mother wanted to become a part of both of their lives.

"I don't want to be English," Emma whispered. "I like my life just the way it is. For months all I've wanted was to be old enough to go to my first *singeon*. Now here I am, on my sixteenth birthday

11

thinking I don't belong. I don't know how to be anyone else other than Amish Emma Byler."

Daniel took off his baseball cap and ran his fingers through his sandy blond hair.

"Nobody says you have to be English," he said. "So, you were born to English parents, but more importantly, you were raised by the Amish who protected you and made you who you are today. I know you can't see it right now, but as I see it, God placed you with the Bylers for a reason. If our mother hadn't given you to Walter Troyer, your Amish uncle, when she did, you would've wound up in a foster home like I did. Who knows if we would have ever found each other?"

Daniel rolled down the window before he continued. "Your life would have been so much different. I count it as a blessing God put you right where He wanted you, right here in Willow Springs, protected and loved. Do I think people may treat you differently when they find out? I surely hope not. You're still Emma Byler, daughter to Jacob and Stella. The girl who always has a smile on her face and goes out of her way to help others. Who you are doesn't change just because you found out you aren't who you thought you were. Look at me. I was born Daniel Cooper, and I spent years bouncing around from one foster home to the next until the Millers adopted me. It didn't make me different because I changed my name. So you see, you're not defined by a name. It's just a name. Emma or Elizabeth, you're still my sister, and Matthew, Rebecca and Anna's sister too. And yes, Jacob and Stella's Emma, and Marie Cooper's Elizabeth."

Letting her absorb all he said, he waited patiently for her to respond or tell him she was ready to move forward.

"I didn't handle it very well when my *datt* tried to explain it all to me this afternoon. I threw my *kapp* on the ground and stormed off like a child. Hearing that my mother was in prison, and my life was nothing but a big fat lie was heart-wrenching. I don't understand how they kept this from me for so long. For months I thought I had done something to upset my *datt*. Here I thought he was mad at me when all along he was nervous about telling me the truth."

12

Tapping his fingers on the steering wheel, Daniel tried to come up with the right words to ease her anxiety.

"I can't know how you feel, but I do know for the last sixteen years I've been mad at our mother," he finally responded. "Hearing your Aunt Anna Mae tell me how Marie begged Walter to take you away opened my eyes to her agony. She knew she was probably going to jail and might never see you again. She saved your life even if you can't see it right now. Just as your Amish parents protected you from the ugliness of the English world, our mother knew your best hope for a good life was with the Amish."

He sighed and looked down at his hands, scarred from a foster home fight he'd had when he was ten. "I don't know what the future will bring for us, but I do know you have two parents at the end of this driveway who are probably worried sick about you. How about you go talk to them and go from there?"

Swallowing the lump in the back of her throat, Emma nodded as Daniel put the truck in Drive and proceeded to take her home.

~~

Pacing the floor in front of the sitting room window, Stella counted seven chimes as the clock echoed from the kitchen. It had been hours since Emma climbed into Daniel's truck and left without a word as to where she was going or if she'd be back. Emma's *kapp* sat cleaned and pressed on Stella's Bible next to her chair. In the kitchen, she heard Rebecca and Anna pulling leftovers out of the refrigerator. She was sure they were trying to busy themselves with dinner while the whole Byler household was on pins and needles. The thickness in the air was suffocating. Even Matthew and Jacob retreated to the barn to escape it. It was as if all life had been drained from the house and it couldn't breathe again until Emma returned.

Stopping at the calendar on the wall near the front door, Stella ran her fingers over the big red circle that announced Emma's birthday. It wasn't her real birthday, but it was the day they celebrated it. Her actual birthday was June seventeenth one month earlier, but no one was ever the wiser except Jacob and her. But now the entire family knew the dark secret they had kept hidden for so long. And soon, with the help of the Amish grapevine, everyone in their community would know as well.

Emma's birthday cake still sat in the middle of the kitchen table, waiting to be enjoyed. No one dare take a bite until Emma came home. Giving in to her tiredness, Stella lowered herself in the chair near the window. Pulling the pale blue pleated curtain aside, her eyes caught movement at the end of the driveway. Walking to the door and out onto the porch she watched as Daniel's truck moved slowly toward her. Thanking *Gott* for answering her prayers, she ran down the stairs and waited for it to come to a complete stop. Holding her breath, she watched, hoping Emma would get out of the truck. For a few minutes, time seemed frozen as she watched her daughter's face for any sign of forgiveness.

Emma looked past her *mamm* and saw her *schwesters* Rebecca and Anna standing on the porch. Out of the corner of her eye, she saw her *datt* and *bruder* standing in the doorway of the barn. Someday was the only one moving, and he was barking and running toward the truck, excited to greet her.

Without moving to open the door, she looked over at Daniel, and before she could say a word, he said, "Emma, this is your family. Look at their faces. Everyone is waiting for you to breathe. You can see it, they love you, and no matter what we've learned today this is where you will always belong. Now go. I'll come back in an hour, and I'll take you to your first singing just like I promised."

Emma took a deep breath and gave him a small smile as she reached for the door handle.

"Thank you for everything. I couldn't have made any sense of what happened today without you. I'm not sure what tomorrow will bring, but today I'll be thankful *Gott* gave me another *bruder*."

Opening the door, she stepped outside and bent down to give Someday a hug. As if on cue, the brown bundle of fur reached up, licked her face and snuggled his muzzle in the crook of her neck. When she looked up, her *mamm* stood in front of her with open arms. Standing, Emma fell into her *mamm's* waiting arms. For a moment the weight of the day floated away in her embrace. Following her *mamm's* lead, she let her guide her into the house as her family fell into step behind them.

Normally her *mamm's* kitchen held all the comforts of home, but at that moment Emma felt like a stranger.

Gripping the back of the chair that had been her place at the table for years, she said, "You all can stop looking at me like that. I'm not going to break."

Rebecca pulled out a chair and sat down. "We were so worried about you. How could you just run off like that?"

"I had a lot to think about, and I couldn't do that here."

"Well, I just don't think it was right for you to worry *Mamm* and *Datt* so much."

Jacob cleared his throat and look sternly at them both. "Sit down," he said. "I have a few things to say."

Without questioning his word, they all sat and waited anxiously to hear what he had to say.

Jacob didn't sit but walked over to the sink and filled a glass of water. Staring out the kitchen window, he said a silent prayer, hoping to find the words his family needed to hear. The decision he made sixteen years ago to bring Emma back to Willow Springs and raise her as their own was now in front of him. Determined not to let it put a wedge in his family, he walked back to the head of the table. Standing behind his chair, he looked into the faces of his family and spoke.

"*Gott* often puts us in situations where we have nowhere left to look but up. This is one of those times. It's been a trying day for all of us. Yes, your *mamm* and I kept the truth about Emma's birth parents a secret and I don't need to explain our reasons for that."

Pulling out his chair, he sat while he contemplated what he was going to say next. His family was waiting on his every word, hoping his leadership would ease their anxiety over what they should expect next.

"I want you all to know Emma will always be your *schwester* and our daughter. That will never change. She has much to think about, and I hope each of you will give her the space she needs to decide what she wants to do. As you all know, her birth mother wants to be a part of her life."

Looking at his youngest daughter, he asked, "Do you have anything you want to say?"

15

Emma couldn't talk if she wanted to. The lump in the back of her throat was restricting her airway, and all she could do was shake her head from side to side. Using the tissue to cover her mouth, she took a deep breath that resulted in a shuddered sob. She couldn't sit there one more minute. The faces looking back at her were full of pity. Pushing herself away from the table, the rubber soles of her black shoes squeaked against the polished wood floor as she ran up the stairs. In the privacy of her room, she threw herself across the bed hoping no one would follow her. She needed a few minutes alone to collect her thoughts and calm the emotions she'd been trying hard to control. Pulling herself up and hugging her knees to her chest, she spotted the wooden box her *datt* had given her earlier. It rested on the hope chest at the foot of her bed. She glared at it, knowing its contents held her other life — one she wasn't sure she wanted to explore. Moving to the end of the bed, she picked it up and held it tight to her chest. Questions were swirling around in her head. *If I open this box, I know there's no going back and what's inside will change my life forever. What is it you want me to do with this, Gott? I'm not sure I'm strong enough to face what is inside.*

She slowly opened the lid, hoping by some small miracle what was inside would have changed from what she saw a few hours ago. Picking up the birth certificate, Emma read the names that clearly stated Jack and Marie Cooper were the birth parents to Elizabeth Marie Cooper born June 17, 2001, in Sugarcreek, Ohio. She reached for the small pink blanket with the initials EMC embroidered in the corner. Holding it to her face, she closed her eyes and tried to imagine herself being wrapped in it. Along with a stack of letters addressed to Elizabeth Cooper was a worn and tattered picture of a small boy holding a baby. Now she knew the boy was Daniel and she was the baby in the photo. Not ready or willing to open the letters, she picked up the newspaper article that went into detail about her mother being arrested for the murder of Jack Cooper. The article talked about the physical abuse and how the judicial system had failed to protect the young woman from a hopeless situation. Closing the lid, she laid back on her bed and tried to imagine what Marie Cooper looked like and what it would have been like to be English. The pounding in her head made her wish she had a cold

16

washcloth to ease the puffiness of her eyes. As if her *mamm* had read her mind, a soft knock on the door resulted in a glass of water, two aspirin, a washcloth, and her head covering.

"Can I come in? I thought you might need these."

"How did you know?"

"A *mamm* always knows what her daughter needs."

"Am I?

"Am I what?" Stella's voice was so loving.

"Am I your daughter? I don't feel like anyone's daughter today. For that matter, I don't feel like I belong anywhere right now."

Pulling herself up and taking the aspirin, she popped them in her mouth and set the glass on the table beside the bed. "I don't want things to change, but I guess I have no say in the matter." Emma's tone was sharp.

Taking Emma's hands in her own and looking deep in her eyes, Stella tried to comfort her hurting daughter the best way she knew how.

"You do have a say. You can take everything you've learned today and decide how you want to handle it. What is best for Emma. *Gott* has given you a path, and you have to trust in Him to walk it with you. You have two families who love you. Who says you have to pick one over the other? Who says you can't have them both? Daniel is more than willing to share you with Matthew and your *schwesters*. Who says your *datt* and I can't share you with Marie Cooper?"

Stella dropped Emma's hands and stroked her cheek. "I don't think your mother wants to change your life; she just wants to get to know you. And lastly, who says you have to figure it all out today? You have a birthday cake sitting downstairs that your *bruder* has been drooling over all day. And don't forget you have a *singeon* to go to tonight that you've been looking forward to for weeks. How about you go wash your face and join your family downstairs for some cake and ice cream?"

Walking toward the door, Stella stopped and turned to say one more thing.

"We're not going to push you into making any decisions. You have to realize our love for you is not going to change. To us, you will always be Emma, and it doesn't matter who you become, you'll always be our daughter."

Watching the door close, Emma reached up to take the hairpins out of her waist-length blonde hair and let it fall around her shoulders. Picking up the hairbrush, she put order back to the unruly locks that had missed the confines of her covering. She twisted it around her fingers and into a bun at the nape of her neck, then secured and positioned the freshly pressed *kapp* to the top of her head. Looking over at the contents of the box on her bed, she scooped it all back inside and placed it under her bed for safekeeping. Pushing it with the toe of her shoe farther under the bed, she said. "Out of sight, out of mind."

Chapter 2 - The Singeon

It was good to hear laughter after such a stressful day. Her older *bruder*, Matthew was telling about one of Rebecca's alpacas spitting on him as he freed it from being tangled in a grapevine. Emma tried to block out everything that had happened that day as she sat surrounded by her family — the only one she knew. The slice of cake Anna put in front of her lost its appeal. She pushed it around with her fork and tried to nibble on it just the same. Listening to everyone talk as if it were an ordinary day, she couldn't help but feel a sense of loss. Was she feeling the loss of her own family or emptiness from a family she didn't know?

"Emma, are you listening?" Anna's voice was tender.

"I'm sorry, were you talking to me?"

"I asked if you are going to the *singeon* with us tonight?"

"Yes. I've invited Daniel to go with us. I hope that's all right?"

Her words were barely out of her mouth when her *datt* spoke up.

"I'm not sure that's a good idea. Why would Daniel want to go to an Amish youth gathering? I don't think it's wise to let him get comfortable spending time with the youth. It's one thing to let Matthew spend so much time with him but inviting him to go with you is taking it a bit too far."

Emma wasn't shocked by her *datt's* reaction. He had made it clear on many occasions he wasn't happy that Daniel and Matthew were friends.

"But *Datt*."

'But, nothing. You're not going to the *singeon* with Daniel tonight, and if you want to go, you'll walk with your *schwesters*, or you'll stay home."

Just then she heard a truck pull up to the house. Standing so she could see out the kitchen window, she said, "That's Daniel."

Jacob pushed his chair back from the table and stood as he hollered over his shoulder. "I'll handle this."

Watching him get up from the table and head to the door, Emma turned toward her *mamm* with pleading eyes.

"I thought it would be fine. After all that has happened today, I had no idea he'd react that way. Didn't he just tell me he was going to let me make my own decisions? He does realize I am going to spend time with him, doesn't he?" Looking hopefully at her *mamm*, Emma waited for her answer.

"I'm sure he is trying to protect you. He's been your *datt* for your whole life, and it's going to take more than a few hours for him to come to terms with you needing to build a relationship with your English family."

Interrupting their conversation, Matthew said. "This is ridiculous," as he got up from the table and grabbed his straw hat off the peg by the back door. "*Datt's* being unfair. Daniel spent more time in Sugarcreek with his Amish friends than he did the English. There is no reason *Datt* should be fearful of our friendship with him. He's Emma's *bruder* and my best friend; that isn't going to change. He's not going to corrupt either one of us. Didn't he just say earlier that this was Emma's choice? She's not going to be able to do that if he forbids her to spend time with him."

Emma didn't know what to think. Walking into the sitting room, she wondered what her *datt* was saying to Daniel. Feeling torn by wanting to obey his wishes but also knowing Matthew was right in saying it was unfair, she had the uncanny feeling that her relationship with Daniel wasn't going to be as easy as she hoped.

~~

Jacob stood on the top step as Daniel got out of truck.

"I'm here to pick up Emma. I promised to take her to the Yoders' tonight."

"I don't think that's a good idea," Jacob said. "Emma has a lot to think about and spending time with you is just going to cloud her judgment. I would prefer you not see her for a while and let her come to terms with things herself."

"I don't mean to disrespect you, sir, but she is my sister, and I want to be there for her."

"I understand that, but as long as she is under my roof, she will obey my wishes, and you have to respect that. She needs time to figure out what she wants to do about meeting your mother. I want her to use good sense and wise counsel, and I can't see how she can do that with your influence."

Daniel didn't know what to say. Part of him wanted to argue with the man, but he understood Jacob's reluctance about the English. It wasn't the first time he'd been made to feel like an outcast by the Amish in Willow Springs. It had been hard trying to fit in with this Old Order Amish Community, and it was better he leave before he made matters worse.

"I will respect your wishes for now, but just so you know I'm not going anywhere. I will be here to help Emma learn about her family when she's ready."

Climbing back in his truck and looking past Jacob, he saw Emma standing in the front window with a worrisome look on her face. He could only imagine what she was going through. Her whole life had been turned upside down, and at that moment, there was nothing he could do. He would honor her father's wishes for now, but he wasn't going to let Emma go through this by herself. Wasn't that what big brothers were for anyway, to protect their younger siblings? It was going to take getting used to, that was for sure. For everyone, including Jacob Byler.

~~

Standing in the doorway of the Yoder's barn, with her older twin *schwesters* on either side, Emma looked out over the faces of her friends. Those she had grown up with and those who had no idea who she really was. For months, Katie Yoder, her best friend, and she had talked of nothing else. The months leading up to their shared birthday, they planned for this very night — the ushering in of their *rumshpringa*. What happened during their running around period

21

was often overlooked by the elders of the church since they had not been baptized yet. It was common knowledge that parents gave their *kinner* the freedom to explore the English world if they wanted. Neither girl was interested in leaving the folds of their Amish community and felt confident they would both take their kneeling vow when they turned eighteen. That was, of course, before Emma learned she wasn't Amish.

Still standing in the doorway as Rebecca and Anna left to mingle with friends their own age, Emma was relieved when Katie ran up to her, grabbed her arm, and pulled her toward the corner of the barn.

"Tell me what was so important that your *datt* made you leave right after the sermon this morning?"

Trying to fight back the tears, Emma sat on a bale of hay, propped her elbows on her knees and rested her chin in her hands. "You're not going to believe it when I tell you," she finally said.

"Samuel said he saw you in Daniel's truck today. What's that all about? He's been pacing the floor all afternoon trying to make sense of why you would be with Daniel, and by yourself at that."

Sitting up straight and kicking her feet out, Emma looked across the barn just as Daniel walked in the back door.

"Wait here, I'll explain it all in a few minutes. I need to talk to Daniel."

Making her way across the barn, she felt everyone in the room was watching her. At that moment she didn't care who saw her or even if her *datt* found out Daniel came to the *singeon*.

Pulling him back outside, she led him to the side of the barn where they could have some privacy.

"What are you doing here? I thought you told my *datt* you weren't coming."

"I know what I said, and I plan on giving you your space just like he requested, but I couldn't sleep until I made sure you were all right."

Grabbing her hand, he placed a small black phone in her palm. "I went to Grove City and picked this up for you. I want you to call me if you need me. If you don't want it, I'll understand."

"*Datt* won't be happy if he finds me with this. I'll need to keep it hidden. You'll need to show me how it works. I only know how to make a call on the phone in the furniture shop."

Leaning in close, he showed her how to turn it on and how to find the programmed number he'd set up. Looking up and over Emma's shoulder, he saw Samuel standing in the shadows of the barn near the door.

"I think you need to go explain to Samuel what's going on. I have a feeling he has the wrong idea about us."

Turning to look over her shoulder, she placed the phone in her pocket and quickly gave Daniel a hug before turning to walk toward Samuel.

Even though the day was nothing to smile about, she couldn't help but be pleased with the look on Samuel's face as she approached him. She thought she saw a bit of jealousy smeared on his brow, which made her insides do a little flip. When she explained everything to him, she was sure she would see him smile again. He'd been through a lot the last couple of months since he'd had his shoulder surgery. The last thing he needed was to think something was going on between her and Daniel. She decided she'd try to lighten his mood before explaining what he'd witnessed.

"Samuel, you don't have your sling on today. Is your shoulder feeling better? I thought you had to wear it for six more weeks."

"My shoulder is fine," he said in an aggravated voice, turning to walk back into the barn.

"Samuel, wait! I need to talk to you about something."

Trying to keep up with his long strides, Emma followed him back inside just as the room had split in two, preparing for the nightly singing. Katie pulled her down in one of the chairs on the girls' side as she passed by. They watched as Samuel walked out of the barn, not stopping to join the group of boys on the opposite side of the room. As one of the older girls started singing the first few words of the first song, Emma jumped up and pulled Katie with her.

"Emma, what are you doing?"

"I need to catch Samuel, and I need to talk to both of you."

Letting go of Katie's hand, she ran after Samuel just as he was climbing up in his open buggy.

"Samuel, please stop."

"I don't think we have anything to talk about. I saw you back there with Daniel Miller. I've been waiting for this night for months, and this is what I get. You sneaking off in a dark corner with that Englisher."

Raising his voice another tone, he said, "I've seen enough – enough that I'm going home."

Shaking her head, smiling, and looking up at him perched high on his buggy seat, she couldn't help but let a little giggle escape her lips. "I don't see what you find so funny," Samuel barked.

Reaching for the reins he had thrown over his horse before climbing up, he pulled the reins back, directing his horse to move backward.

Jumping back just in time to escape the wooden buggy wheel from going over her foot, she yelled.

"Daniel Miller is my *bruder!*"

Katie had since caught up to her and pulled her around to face her as she repeated.

"Daniel Miller is your *bruder?* What on earth are you talking about? Why would you say such a thing? He's English, and Matthew is your *bruder*. You're Emma Byler, not Emma Miller."

Stopping his horse from going any further, Samuel secured the reins and jumped down off his seat. "What are you talking about? You're not making any sense. How about you start from the beginning and tell us what's going on."

"Not here," Emma said, "can we leave? I don't feel much like singing tonight anyways."

"Just so I'm clear," Samuel said. "Nothing is going on between you and Daniel?"

Emma reached in her pocket and pulled out the phone. "Not unless you call him giving me a phone is something going on."

"Looking at it from the outside I would say a phone is something going on," Samuel replied. "Why would he give you that unless he wants you to call him?"

"It's a long story, but to begin with my *datt* has forbidden him to see me and he wanted to be sure I had a way to get in touch with him if I need him."

"Okay, this is getting too far-fetched for me to understand. Let's go find somewhere to talk. Katie, you might as well come with us. It's not how I had planned this evening to go but, if you say there isn't anything going on between the two of you, I will at least hear you out."

Walking past Emma to climb up in the buggy, Katie whispered in her ear. "I'm sure he had big plans to drive you home tonight. He spent all day yesterday washing this buggy. I'm sure he's not too happy he's taking his first ride with you with me tagging along."

Katie's whisper wasn't so quiet that Samuel couldn't hear it.

"That's all right," she said, "you both need to hear what I have to say anyways."

Samuel backed the buggy up and turned it around to head down the driveway. "Left or right?"

Emma pointed right. "How about we go to Willow Bridge? There won't be much traffic there until the *singeon* is over. That will give us a good place to stop and talk for a few minutes."

As Samuel guided his courting buggy toward the covered bridge, he was full of questions about what Emma had just shared with them. He didn't want to push her into explaining more than she was ready for and waited patiently for her to start talking.

Emma sat silently with her hands folded on her lap, playing the day's events over and over in her head.

As they turned onto Willow Bridge Road, Emma saw Daniel's truck parked in the field next to Willow Bridge.

"For sure and certain that's Daniel's truck," Samuel said as he nodded his head in the direction of the bridge.

"I wonder why he's parked out here all by himself," Emma asked more for herself than expecting an answer from anyone.

Pulling the buggy up beside Daniel, Samuel stopped in line with the driver's side window so he could speak to Daniel face-to-face. "I hear you and Emma have quite a story to tell."

Bracing his arms on the steering wheel, Daniel looked past Samuel toward Emma. "That we do. If you're up to it."

25

Nodding her head, she watched as Samuel tied his horse off to a nearby tree and reached for her hand to help her down from the buggy. Without waiting to be helped, Katie climbed out. *I know how I rate when Emma's around,* she thought. Smiling to herself, she couldn't be mad. She had known for months that Samuel and Emma had a soft spot for each other and could only guess of her *bruder's* plans for the evening. One that didn't include his baby *schwester*.

Unlatching the truck's tailgate, Daniel patted its surface, indicating they should all sit. Seeing how far it was from the ground, Samuel didn't think twice before putting his hands around Emma's waist to lift her up. Dropping her before he even got a good hold of her, he flinched in pain as he let her go. "Well, that's not going to happen. I guess my shoulder's not ready for lifting yet."

Without missing a beat, Daniel lifted Katie up and then turned and did the same for Emma. Standing on the ground and leaning on the tailgate next to Katie, Daniel looked toward Emma. "Do you want to start, or should I?"

"I've done enough talking today – you go ahead," Emma said, her voice drained.

For the next thirty minutes, Daniel explained how he and Matthew had gone to Sugarcreek to look for his sister. How the Millers had adopted him after he'd spent years in foster care and how his biological mother was serving a prison term for voluntary manslaughter. He explained how they had stopped at Matthew's aunt's house only to find her address was the same his mother had given him to start his search. But most of all, he explained that his long-lost sister, Elizabeth, was right under his nose all along. She was safe and sound, tucked deep inside the Amish community in Willow Springs as Emma Byler. By the time he was done, Katie was crying, and Samuel had reached over and taken Emma's hand, rubbing his thumb across her knuckles trying to soothe her.

"I'm sorry I jumped to conclusions when I saw you both out by the barn," Samuel said. "I should have known there was more to the story than what I saw."

Daniel chuckled. "I'm sure if I were in your shoes, I would have thought the same thing. But you can rest assured my only interest in Emma is as her brother."

They all laughed, and it helped lighten the mood after the profound story they had just shared.

"That isn't the whole story. Not only does our mother want to see us, but she also wants to be a part of our lives. On top of that, Jacob has forbidden me to see or talk to Emma. I think he's afraid I will pull her away from him and into the sordid past of her newfound family. I can tell you all, that is the last thing I want to do. Emma, you're going to have to make your own mind up about how much or how little you want our mother to be in your life. I will not sway you either way. I only gave you that phone so you'll have a way to talk to me if you so choose. I may be your big brother, but this is all on you. One way or another, I'll do what you want — no questions asked. I've spent a good part of my life mad at my mother for the choices she made, but as I get older and understand more, I can see she did what she felt was best for the both of us. Even if that meant handing you off to a stranger."

They all sat quietly for a few minutes, letting the warm summer breeze swirl around them. They listened to the peepers and a distant owl playing a nighttime song. The moon's beams were bouncing off Willow Creek, giving them just enough light to see each other's faces.

"Emma, I made a promise to your *datt* and I attend to keep it. Now that I know you are in good hands with Samuel and Katie, I should be going. I would hate anyone to see us

together, and it get back to your parents. I need to earn their trust, and I am not going to do that by going behind their back and seeing you."

Sliding off the tailgate, Emma laid her hand on Daniel's forearm. "Thank you. I couldn't have made it through today without you. I feel blessed to not only have one older *bruder* but two." She patted the phone in her pocket. "I will call you if I need to talk."

Following Emma, Katie jumped off the tailgate and ran around the side of the truck. "Daniel, do you mind driving me home? I'm sure my big *bruder* would rather his little *schwester* not tag along on his first buggy ride with Emma."

Chapter 3 - Sarah

Pulling Sarah's letter out of his pocket and resting his elbows on the fence, Matthew started to replay the last few days in his head. It'd been only a week since Daniel, and he had returned home from Sugarcreek. So much had happened. Daniel found Elizabeth, and he found Sarah on her brother-in-law's farm. The agonizing year he'd spent waiting for any word from her dissolved the minute he looked into her eyes. Not understanding why Sarah felt she couldn't confide her fears of leaving her *schwester's kinner* and why they couldn't tell Nathan about their relationship troubled him. But he prayed they would be able to figure out a solution for her being in Sugarcreek while he was in Willow Springs. The offer her brother-in-law, Nathan Bouteright, had given him was appealing. Nathan had offered him a job as a stable hand so he could learn about the horse business. Nathan was looking for a farm in northwestern Pennsylvania he could use as a holding stable for local buyers. That was, however, before they left Sugarcreek so abruptly, without so much of an explanation. Now he wasn't sure he could leave his family. Emma spent most of her days closed up in her room while his parents tried to act like nothing had changed. One thing he knew for sure. He needed to talk to Daniel, and he needed to find a way to get his *datt* to lighten up on Emma. As he saw it, forbidding her to see Daniel only made matters worse.

Pulling the flowery stationery out of the envelope, Matthew unfolded the letter. Sarah's handwriting comforted him. She always did have perfect penmanship, while his own looked more like chicken scratch.

My Dearest Matthew,

Hello from a warm and sunny Tuesday afternoon in Sugarcreek. The weather has been mild this week, no rain so far. I've been able to pick the last of the green beans from the garden and a few peppers. Nathan got in a few new horses this morning, and all the stable hands are busy getting them settled. Amos is down for a nap and Rachel is sitting out on the porch with Rosie. Gott has been good to us this week.

I suspect you made it back to Willow Springs safely. I hope whatever you had to take care of at home has been resolved. I still can't believe you found me. I don't know what I was thinking by not telling you where I was. Please forgive me for not going to you and having faith we could figure things out together. I was in such a dilemma about leaving Rachel and Amos. Ever since Susan died, I have not been able to think of anything else but her kinner. Susan and I made a promise years ago after our own mamm died that we would always be there for each other. By caring for her kinner, I felt I was keeping that promise. Nathan walked around in a daze for months, and I just didn't have the heart to leave them. I know we'd made plans to marry, but how could I marry you and take care of the kinner at the same time? I couldn't figure it out. Again, why I didn't just go to you in the first place is beyond me. The day I saw your face in the garden, I knew I'd made a big mistake. I miss you and am praying for your safe return to Sugarcreek. I hope Gott will send you back to me and you will accept Nathan's offer to work here for a couple months. That will give us time to figure it all out.

All my love,
Sarah

Folding the letter and placing it back in the envelope, Matthew tucked it in his back pocket just as the sound of the feed delivery truck turned down the driveway. Walking to the barn, he opened the double doors so they could carry the feed inside. Waiting as the green box truck circled the driveway and stopped beside him, Matthew stepped forward to close the distance between them.

"I wondered when I'd see you again."

"I've tried to stay away like your dad asked me to. But you're on my delivery route, so he'll have to excuse this visit."

Without getting out of the truck, he looked toward the Furniture Shop, making sure Jacob was nowhere in earshot.

"How is Emma? I've been worried about her. Just so you know I gave her a phone to call me if she needed to talk, but so far she hasn't used it."

"She's been spending a good bit of time in her room. We've been trying to give her some space. Nobody knows what to say to her. I'm not too happy my father has forbidden you to talk to her. I think you are exactly what she needs right now."

"I do too."

"Well, let's get this feed unloaded so I can get out of here before I overstay my welcome."

~~

Sipping his coffee, Jacob stood at the shop window watching Matthew talk to Daniel. He wondered what they were talking about. No doubt, it was Emma. No matter what he wanted, he couldn't deny Matthew and Daniel were friends. Was he wrong in not allowing Emma to speak to him? What was he so afraid of? The pressure of all that had happened was taking its toll on his family. Stella was looking tired, and just that morning, she didn't get up with him for the first time in years. The twins kept to themselves, and Matthew spent most of his days in the barn. Emma hadn't said a word to him in over a week, and even Someday, their chocolate lab, acted like he was mad at him. When the dog wouldn't warm up to him, something was amiss. Maybe it was time he went to see the Bishop.

~~

Emma heard Daniel's truck shift gears on Mystic Mill Road long before she saw it pull down the driveway and park in front of the barn. Standing at her bedroom window, the warm summer breeze floated around her like a comforting hug. Looking out over the garden below and the weeds that were on the verge of consuming it,

31

she decided to go tackle them instead of staying locked in her room a minute longer. She'd spent the morning staring at the letters from her mother, trying to force herself to read what was inside. The overwhelming feeling that the minute she opened them she'd lose her Amish identity kept her from breaking the seal.

She'd yet changed from her nightgown into the dark blue work dress that hung on the peg beside her bed. Pinning her hair up and slipping on her dress, Emma quickly used straight pins to close the bodice, before grabbing a blue headscarf from the top drawer of her dresser. Tying the cloth under her chin as she walked down the hall, she passed by her parents' room, in time to hear her *mamm* call out to her.

"Emma, is that you?" Stella's voice sounded weak.

Stopping and gently pushing the door open, Emma saw Stella still in bed with a quilt pulled up tight around her chin.

"*Mamm* what's the matter, are you feeling ill?"

"I must have caught a little bug or something. Will you go find the hot water bottle and bring it up to me?"

"Of course, I'll be right back. Is there anything else I can get you? A cup of tea or some toast?"

"No, just the hot water bottle. I think I might need to stay put. I would hate for anyone else to come down with this."

"Certainly, I'll be right back."

Running down the steps, her bare feet took them two at a time trying to get back to her *mamm* quickly.

In the kitchen, Rebecca was kneading bread at the counter. "So, you decided to join us. It's about time you left your room. I'm getting sick of doing all of your chores. I know *Mamm* and *Datt* told us to leave you alone, but enough is enough."

Emma could always count on Rebecca to tell it like it was. She was always the one to point out her indiscretions. Why should today be any different?

"I don't need your sarcasm right now. Do you know *Mamm* is not feeling well?"

"I do, why do you think I'm in the house making bread and Anna's downstairs doing laundry instead of being at the Flea Market selling our yarn? If you had been anywhere but locked in your room for the last week, you would have known she hasn't been herself all week long."

Opening the cupboard under the sink, Emma stooped down, rummaging through the cleaning products looking for the blue rubber bottle. Pulling it out from behind the well-worn dishpan, she stood, flipped the water on, and grabbed the tea kettle off the stove. Filling it to the top and placing it on the back of the stove, she opened the firebox and added kindling. Waiting for the fire to take hold, she held her hand over the burner and moved the kettle once she felt the heat.

"While the water is heating, I'm going outside to talk to Daniel."

"You know *Datt's* not going to like that."

"You don't need to tell me that. I know he'll probably be watching from the shop, and I'll hear his wrath later, but I need to talk to my *bruder*."

Letting the screen door slam, she ran out through the mudroom and rounded the house just in time to see Daniel pull away from the barn.

Choosing not to run after him, she stopped and watched as the Feed & Seed truck pulled out of the driveway and onto Mystic Mill Road. She assumed he was headed back to the Co-op at the edge of town.

Feeling for the phone in her pocket, Emma found her need to talk to Daniel getting stronger. She would need to find a place she could safely use it out of earshot of her family. Being forbidden to speak to the only person who understood what she was going through was suffocating.

Walking back in the kitchen, she gently laid her hand on the side of the kettle, checking to see if the water had warmed enough to fill the bottle on the counter. Deciding it needed a few more minutes, she walked to the sink to wash the dishes Rebecca had used to make bread and breakfast. Trying to ignore Rebecca's snippy looks, she felt relief when Anna walked up the stairs with a basket of clothes balanced on her hip. Even though her twin sisters looked the same, their personalities were completely opposite. Rebecca was never afraid to speak her mind; Anna, though, had a quiet and gentle spirit that was comforting the minute she walked in the room.

"Emma, it's good to see you downstairs."

"I decided I needed some air, so I'm going to weed the garden. I've neglected it this week, and the weeds are about to take over," she replied. "I am pretty sure the green beans are about done, but we should plan a day to can beets. *Mamm* said we needed to make pickled beets this year. I checked last week, and we still have plenty of regular beets to last the winter. I will ask her about them when I take the hot water bottle up to her."

"Is she still not feeling well?" Anna asked. "*Datt* let her sleep in this morning."

"She called for me when I passed her room and asked for the hot water bottle. As soon as I take it up to her, I'll be going out to the garden. She said she thinks she caught a little bug."

"I bet she is under the weather because of all the drama you've put her through the last week or so," Rebecca chimed in.

"Drama I put her through!" Emma said in a voice louder than she had expected.

Grabbing the potholder off the hook on the side of the stove, Emma picked up the tea kettle and headed to the sink.

Still talking louder than she should be, she said, "I'd say I didn't have much say in all the drama this family has endured this week."

Filling the rubber bottle and setting the kettle down inside the porcelain sink, she turned around only to see her *datt* standing in the doorway separating the sitting room from the kitchen.

Rebecca and Anna turned to where Emma was looking and stood in complete silence.

"What's going on in here?" Jacob said harshly. "I could hear your voices out on the porch. All of you know your *mamm* is not feeling well and the last thing she needs to hear is the three of you arguing like a bunch of barn cats. Anna, get those clothes on the line. Rebecca, finish that bread so you can get outside and take care of those alpacas. Emma, that garden needs your attention so get to it. Is that for your mother?"

"Yes, sir."

"Give it to me, I'll take it up to her. I came in to check on her anyways."

"Now get going, and I don't want to have to come in here again."

~~

As quietly as he could, Jacob opened their bedroom door trying not to wake Stella if she'd gone back to sleep. Standing over her, he noticed she looked flushed. Holding the back of his hand to her forehead, she felt warm to his touch. Startled, Stella opened her eyes and patted the side of the bed for him to sit.

"What was all the racket downstairs?" Stella tried to pull herself up on the bed.

"Just girls being girls. I'm sure Rebecca's snippy comments and Emma's anxiousness just clashed." Jacob's voice was tender. "You don't worry about it. I can handle our girls on my own."

Stella reached for the glass of water on the nightstand. "That's what I'm worried about. Your patience is worn pretty thin these days, and it wouldn't take much for you to lash out at any one of them."

"They're almost adults now, and each one of them can take care of themselves, even when I come down on them hard. My job isn't to make them like me, my job is to make them into *Ordnung* abiding adults. I'll be their friend after they've left this house and have families of their own."

"Oh, Jacob, if only they all knew what a softy you really are. Someday when we have grandchildren of our own, they will see what a teddy bear you really are."

"Well, none of them need to figure that out right now. I still have years of rearing ahead of me. So, you keep that little secret between the two of us."

Jacob took his wife's hand. "Now, let's talk about that fever you have going on. You haven't been yourself for weeks. I can see you've pushed yourself each day only to go to bed by eight o'clock. I think it's time we take a trip to the doctors."

"It's just a little bug," Stella demurred. "The water bottle is for this sore spot I have under my arm. I must have hit it on something because it's tender. I think it needs some warmth to take the soreness away. The fever is nothing, and I am probably warm from being under all these quilts in the middle of summer. I'm just feeling out of sorts. Give me a few days, and I'll be back to my old self in no time at all."

"I'll let you go just a couple more days, and that's it." Jacob leaned down and kissed her on the cheek. "You stay right here and get better. I'll keep the *kinner* under control, and I promise I'll watch my temper until you get better to soften my blows."

He pulled the door closed and headed down the stairs to make sure the girls had followed his instructions. The house was empty. The only sound he heard was the clicking of the clock that hung above the kitchen sink. The girls made it a point to be long gone before he came back downstairs. A little part of him felt bad they scattered like grasshoppers any time he was near. And for that matter, he couldn't blame them. It had been obvious he'd been difficult to get along with the last year or so. But again he didn't need to explain himself to anyone but *Gott* and Stella.

~~

Sitting in the middle of the garden, surrounded by a pile of weeds, Emma cleared her head by digging her hands in the warm soil. With each unwanted plant she pulled from around the beets, she felt a little stronger. Sitting out in the hot sun with sweat trickling down the back of her neck, she felt braver about removing the pink ribbon that held her birth mother's words so tight. Part of her wanted to read them with Daniel close by, but the other part of her wanted to be alone with the letters that were meant for her. Maybe after supper she'd walk down to the creek that ran through the back of the farm. Patting her pocket to make sure the phone was still securely hidden, she thought it would be safe to call Daniel from there. For now, she would be comforted in immersing herself in one of her favorite jobs, gardening.

36

Chapter 4 - The Letters

Pushing the wheelbarrow full of weeds out behind the barn, Emma stopped at the fence to feed a handful of sweet clover to one of Rebecca's alpacas. Rebecca and Anna spent all of their extra time caring for the pack of fiber-giving creatures. Their large wraparound porch was constantly filled with rack after rack of dyed alpaca fiber. During the summer they would wash, dry and dye it so they could spend the winter months spinning it into skeins of beautiful soft yarn. Often, they spun the fine strands with wool to make it stronger and more versatile. She, on the other hand, had no desire to work with the ill-tempered animals. Emma would rather spend her time helping Katie with their budding bakery business.

Before this business with Marie Cooper, they had been planning to convince the Bishop to allow them to start their own bakery. They had already drawn up plans for Katie's *datt* to expand the Strawberry Stand, which included a new kitchen. However, the Bishop had yet to approve their new venture. With both of them just completing their schooling last year, he felt they weren't old enough to run a business. "Give it a few more months," Katie's *datt* had told them. "Then I'll talk to him again." Until then, they were given permission to keep using Katie's *mamms'* kitchen to fill their growing orders.

Leaning the emptied wheelbarrow against the barn, she turned on the outside spigot to wash the dirt from her hands. She was in no hurry to help Rebecca with dinner and even less to sit at the table with her *datt*. Shaking the excess water from her hands, she wiped them on her dress before heading around to the front of the barn. Matthew came around the barn just as she turned the corner.

"Whoa, watch it little *schwester*. It would help if you picked your chin up off the ground so you could see where you're going."

"Sorry, I wasn't paying attention." Emma looked over Matthew's shoulder to be sure *Datt* was nowhere in sight. "Did Daniel say anything to you this morning about me?" she whispered. "I tried to get out of the house to talk to him, but I was helping *mamm* with something and missed him."

Taking his hat off his head and wiping his brow with the back of his sleeve, Matthew said.

"You know *Datt* won't be happy if he sees you talk to him."

"So, did he ask about me?"

"He did. He told me about the phone. You'd better keep that out of sight if you don't want *Datt* going off on you again."

"I will, I'm not that stupid. I haven't even turned it on yet. I already got hollered at once today. I'm not looking for a repeat performance."

"Give him some time. He's not always been as uptight as he's been lately. I bet once he figures out he can't stop you from seeing Daniel or even talking to your birth mother he'll back off."

"I have so many questions that only Daniel can answer, but I'm afraid of what I might learn."

Letting a few moments pass between them before he spoke, Matthew chose his words carefully.

"Life wasn't meant to be easy," he finally said. "I have to believe *Gott* puts challenges in front of us to make us rely on Him more. If we didn't have our faith, where would we be?"

Picking up a stick off the ground and taking out his pocketknife, Matthew rested a bended knee on the barn. Peeling the bark off the end of the stick, he continued in a hushed tone.

"You have to remember, you're in your *rumshpringa*, and *Datt* really has no hold on you. Yes, he's going to try to keep you under his thumb, but ultimately it is your decision how far you want to go with all of this."

Leaning up against the weathered whitewashed barn, Emma tipped her head back so she was looking up to the sky.

"But what if I make the wrong choice?"

"What choice do you have to make? You can continue to live here in our sheltered community always wondering what your other family is like. Or, you can step out of your little box and go find out for yourself. It's a choice only you can make."

"My stomach is all in knots. I don't know what I want."

"Give it time. No one says you have to figure it out in a week."

"Thanks. I guess I'd better go help with dinner. *Datt* will be in soon, and I want to check on *mamm*."

"Anytime."

As she started to walk to the house, he grabbed her arm and whispered. "Keep that phone hidden. I won't be able to lie to *Datt* if he asks if I knew anything about it."

~~

Emma tried to be as helpful as she could without getting in anyone's way. She worked side-by-side with Rebecca and Anna to finish making dinner and doing the rest of *Mamm's* chores for the day. Not wanting to upset either of their parents, they all kept to themselves as best as they could. At twelve o'clock on the nose, both Matthew and Jacob came in for dinner.

Going to the sink to wash his hands, Jacob asked, "Has anyone checked on your *mamm* lately?"

"I took her up a cup of tea and a slice of toast a few minutes ago," Anna responded, bringing a platter of roasted chicken to the table. "She told me she wouldn't be coming down to dinner and to go ahead and eat without her."

Drying his hands on the towel by the sink, Jacob went to the head of the table without another word. Bowing their heads for the silent prayer, they all waited for him to clear his throat before filling their plates. Afraid to say as much as a word, all three girls ate in silence.

Matthew filled the void by talking about how much the soybeans had grown and how funny the alpacas look since being sheared.

Emma, on the other hand, couldn't wait to finish eating so she could go back outside and away by herself. All she wanted to do was figure out a way to carry her box to the creek and call Daniel.

Finally, Jacob pushed himself away from the table. "I'm going to go check on your *mamm,*" he said. "While I do that, Matthew, hitch up the wagon. We need to deliver new tables to the Apple Blossom Inn. We have a few errands to run in town, so we'll be gone most of the afternoon. I expect all of you to get your chores done before I get back."

Emma raised an eyebrow and thought to herself. *Good. Maybe I can take a walk and won't have to wait until after supper to sneak off.*

Not wasting any time cleaning up the kitchen, Emma retreated to her room, while the twins headed outside to the barn.

The house was finally quiet, and all that could be heard in Emma's room was a bird chirping outside the window. Reaching for the box she had pushed far under her bed that morning, Emma sat with it on her lap. Opening the lid, she pulled out the stack of letters addressed to Elizabeth Cooper with her aunt Anna Mae's address on them. The return address was a Mayfield, Ohio address that wasn't familiar. She assumed it was the address of the Women's Prison.

Rubbing the pink ribbon between her fingers, Emma felt her stomach churn. She knew it was now or never. Putting the stack on her nightstand, she closed the lid and slid the box back under her bed for safekeeping. Grabbing the small lap quilt at the foot of her bed, she held the letters and covered them with the little blanket across her arm. She didn't want anyone to see what she was carrying. Tiptoeing past her parents' room, she took each step downstairs softly, trying to remember which step creaked under her weight. Making it to the door, she opened the screen slowly to keep it from squeaking. Outside, she looked to the barn to see if Rebecca or Anna would notice she was leaving. Not that they would care where she was going, she just didn't want anyone to know where she had gone. Finally getting far enough away from the house she could uncover the stack of letters, she shifted the blanket to the other arm.

Walking down the path that led to the creek, Emma took in all the sights and sounds of summer. Old maple trees lined the tractor path that provided her shade. Many times she and Katie would walk this path to spend a lazy afternoon wading in Willow Creek. Today its comforting banks would give her the privacy she needed to meet her mother through her letters.

Finding the perfect spot to spread out the quilt, she placed the stack of letters down along with the phone from her pocket. As *kinner*, they would sing a little song as they sat. Without anyone around, she sang as she lowered herself on the blanket.

"Criss-Cross Applesauce. Give your hands a clap. Criss-Cross Applesauce. Put them in your lap.

"How silly of me," she said out loud. "I'm not a child anymore." But she smiled just the same with the memory it brought back.

Picking up the letters, Emma gently untied the ribbon and took her time to look at each one. Each was postmarked on the 17th of June. Sixteen in all. Trying to decide which one to open first, she pulled the last one from the stack and placed the rest aside. Taking a deep breath, she turned it over and slid her finger under the flap. Unfolding it and trying to get used to the angle of her mother's writing, she read the first line a few times before moving on.

June 17, 2002

My Dearest Daughter,

Today is your first birthday, and my thoughts are only of you. My heart aches to hold you and to smell your sweet baby fragrance. Our time together was cut short, and I feel I barely got to know you before our lives were separated. I hope wherever you are, you are well cared for. I am finding it hard to imagine what you look like. If you favor your brother, your big brown eyes and fuzzy blonde hair has captured the hearts of your new family. I'm comforted that you were too little to remember who I was. Too little to miss your mother's embrace, before you settled into your new mother's arms.

You are much too young for me to explain why I am away from you. So, for now just know I love you more than life. Please be a good girl, and I hope someday our paths will cross again.

All my love,
Momma

Tears streaming down her face, Emma wasn't sure she could read all sixteen letters. The pain she felt from her mother's words dug deep into the sudden understanding of the pain she must have felt giving her away. She had to read more. She had to know what pushed her to kill her father. She had to relive her mother's life through her eyes.

June 17, 2003

My Dearest Elizabeth,

Two years. I have missed so much. I am sure by now, you are walking and putting some words together. I hope you are enjoying summer. Daniel loved playing outside. We went to the park shortly after you were born, and we played catch while you slept in your car seat. Every few minutes, he had to go check on you to make sure you were all right. He was such a good big brother. He loved you so much. Someday I hope you'll get to meet him. I am not sure you are getting these letters, and even if you do, you are much too young to understand who I am. If someone is reading this to you, please know I have kissed each of these words and sent them all to you in this letter. The day I get to see you again, I promise to cover you in so many mommy kisses you'll never miss them ever again.
Someday, baby, I promise I'll hold you again,
Love, Momma

Folding the last letter up and tucking it back in the envelope, she uncrossed her legs and stretched out on the small blanket. Closing her eyes, she let the sun beat down on her, hoping the warmth would clear her mind. How was she ever going to get through all sixteen letters in one sitting? She could hear the agony in her mother's words. She didn't have children of her own, but the thought of not being able to be near a child she gave birth to was unbearable. Is this what her parents were going through with the possibility she would leave them? Sitting back up, she pulled the next letter from the stack. Each one contained a heartfelt message much like the one before. Some described what it was like not knowing where her children were, and others explained her life behind the steel bars that kept her from them. One thing was clear, though. Her mother had lost all hope in *Gott*. Emma worked through each letter until she reached the last one that Aunt Anna Mae had passed on to her *datt*.

June 17, 2017

Elizabeth,

My heart aches for you. Today is your sixteenth birthday. The day when most young girls step into the folds of young womanhood. I have no idea where you are or what became of you. For the last sixteen years, I've sent a letter to the same address I left you at in Sugarcreek. The Amish man I gave you to promised that he would tell you of me on this day. Has that happened? What do you know of me? Please know I have tried to find you. I even begged your brother to look for you.

Daniel is a young man now. He is living in a small town in Pennsylvania called Willow Springs. At this point, he hasn't wanted too much to do with me. I can't say I don't blame him. I have failed my children, I have failed God, and I have failed myself. Will you ever forgive me, Elizabeth?

Today is the day I tell you about your past. About the father you never got to know, about the grandmother who would have loved you until I returned and about me.

Your father was the most handsome man I had ever met. We met at the restaurant I was working at in Sugarcreek. He came in every day at lunch and sat in my section. I was only sixteen myself when we first met. His straw hat and brown eyes captivated me from the very beginning. If you don't know much about Sugarcreek, let me explain. It is one of the largest Amish communities in the country. Yes, your father was Amish.

My father was Amish! Emma could hardly believe what she had read. How could that be? The knot in her stomach got tighter as she continued to read her mother's letter. She giggled as she read the next line.

43

You may not know much about the Amish, but they go through a period in their life called rumshpringa. A time when they can go out and explore more worldly things. To your father, Jake, I was one of those worldly things he could explore. Not only did he chase me, but he also discovered beer. So much so that his father kicked him out of his house and disowned him. He swore he'd never go back to his father's house again. He was so mad he changed his name and dropped all ties to his Amish community. He partied a lot back then, and I hoped it was just a phase that he'd grow out of. The group of English boys he hung around with were bad news. I begged him to leave them and go back to his family, but he wouldn't. The drinking got worse, the bruises got more severe, and then I got pregnant. I felt my only choice was to marry your father when he asked. I am sure he asked more out of duty to his upbringing then wanting a wife and baby. After that, it went from bad to worse. His drinking binges got so bad that at times, he took them out on me. Please believe me when I say I tried to go to the police, but they couldn't or wouldn't help. All it did was make him madder. The day we ended up on that back road in Amish country, I had to make a quick decision. It was him or the Amish man he hit with the crowbar. There was no way I could let a man lose his life because of the choices I made.

Emma stopped reading. "That was my *Datt*," she said, though no one could hear her.

Your Grandmother. My world and the lifeblood of our family. Being sent to prison killed her. She begged me to leave your father, but I felt it my duty to try to help him. The strain of our vile relationship took such a toll on her we stopped talking for years. She had not even met you before I was taken from you. She was given custody of Daniel but only was able to keep him for a short time before she died. I miss her so. My own father died in an accident when I was five. I admire that she took me to church every Sunday and work two jobs to support us. I never went without, and I always knew God.
I'm so far from that person now I'm not sure I'll ever be able to go back. God has abandoned me. I've lost my son, I've lost my

mother, but most of all I have failed you. Will God ever show up in my life again?

Emma wiped the tears from her face on a corner of the quilt. "Oh Momma," she said, "*Gott* hasn't abandoned you. He's there. You'll see, I'll show you."

This is the last letter I will be writing to you. I am hoping by now Daniel will have gone to Sugarcreek and found out anything he could about your whereabouts. In two months, I'll be released from this place. Maybe by some small miracle, we will meet again.

I can't leave this world without seeing your face just one more time. I promise if you don't want to get to know me, I will respect your wishes. But please, Elizabeth let me look into your eyes one last time and tell you how sorry I am for leaving you.
Always my love,
Momma

Not even taking the time to put the letter away, she picked up the phone, turned it on and pressed the number one to call Daniel.

He answered on the second ring.

"Emma, is that you?"

Without even saying hello, she said, "Our father was Amish."

Chapter 5 - At the Creek

Parking his truck in the field beside the covered bridge, Daniel climbed over the guardrail and down the bank to the path that curved around Willow Creek. Emma told him where he could find her and she promised to stay put until he got there. It took him almost an hour to finish his deliveries and exchange his work truck for his own after she called. The two-minute conversation didn't give him enough information on all she had learned in the letters. Picking up his pace, he jogged along the bank of the creek looking for the place Emma described.

~~

Placing the last of the letters back in its matching envelope, Emma stood and wiped her face on the back of her sleeve. Walking to the creek, she knelt down and splashed water on her swollen eyes. Making it through all of the letters was harder than she imagined. Each one revealed a bit more about her mother's anguish, about the life she led outside of prison and the one she endured behind bars. If nothing else, they helped her feel closer to the woman she had never met. Opening her eyes, she looked down at the reflection in the water. The face she saw was Emma Byler, the young Amish girl with a life that had been planned out for her long ago. However, the person inside was becoming more like Elizabeth Cooper, the young English girl with a broken family. Studying the image, she felt surer about what she needed to do next. Hearing footsteps, she stood and waited for Daniel to come into sight.

Stopping within a yard of her, he leaned over and rested his hands on his knees while he caught his breath.

"Thank you for coming," Emma said. "I hope you didn't get in trouble for leaving work early."

"It was no problem. I was finishing my last delivery when you called."

Walking to the quilt, Emma pointed to it, inviting him to sit. She handed him the stack of letters. "You need to read these."

"I couldn't do that, they're yours."

"No, I want you to. Did she write you letters too?"

"In the beginning, she did. I was young, and they were upsetting me, so my caseworker told her to stop. Once she signed over her parental rights to the Millers, I didn't get many more. When I got older, she started to send them again. The most recent ones all said the same thing. Find you. If it weren't for my dad, I wouldn't have responded back to her."

Emma leaned back on her hands and looked out over the creek. Finally, she spoke.

"You need to read these letters. We need to help her, not shut her out."

"What do you mean? What do we need to help her with?"

"Do you remember when we went for ice cream the night I found out who I was and you told me that God put us on this path for a reason? You told me we both have a lot of forgiving to do, and maybe God wants us to help Marie. After everything I've read, I have to believe you're right. I've been thinking about how amazing it is that God placed you with Christian parents and me with the Amish. He had this all planned long before we ever knew. Our mother is lost, and we need to help her. Please read these."

Opening the first letter he did as she asked. He read through each letter without saying a word. When he got to the last one, he folded it neatly back in its envelope and handed the stack back to her.

"I don't know what to say. I never gave much thought to what she may have gone through all of these years. I guess guys just don't think like that. All I knew was I missed my mother, and I blamed her for leaving me. My grandmother tried to explain things to me, but I guess I was too little to really understand."

Daniel paused, gathering his thoughts. "So how do you propose we help her?"

47

"She wrote that she was being released next month. Can we bring her here to Willow Springs to live?"

"I doubt she'll be able to leave Ohio. Dad said most likely she'll be on probation and won't be able to leave the area."

Emma turned to him. "Then we need to go to Sugarcreek." Her voice was determined.

"Sugarcreek? Are you sure? Jacob is never going to allow that."

"He's not going to like it. But just like Matthew reminded me this morning, I'm on my rumshpringa, and there isn't much he can do about it. Whether I choose to stay Amish or not, I haven't been baptized, and I'm free to make whatever choice I want. I won't be banned or forbidden to see my family, so this is the best time to leave Willow Springs."

"But what about Samuel?"

"Samuel and I have been friends for a long time, and he knows I've got a lot going on right now. I'm sure if I talk to him, he'll give me his blessing. I'm not sure I want to move there permanently, but for now, our mother needs us. Can we go?"

"I'll need to talk to my folks and my boss first. If you're sure that's what you want?"

"I'm sure."

Daniel pushed himself up off the quilt and reached for Emma's hand to help her up.

"I guess we're going to Ohio," he said.

"That's the easy part. Telling my *datt* is another story."

"Can I give you a ride back home?"

"You'd better not. Let me break it to my parents first before they see us together again. I think I'm going to cut through the strawberry fields and see if I can talk to Samuel."

Picking up the letters, not caring to conceal them under the quilt, Emma waved goodbye to Daniel. As she walked away, she patted the phone in her pocket and told him she would call him tomorrow.

~~

Walking beside the row of sugar maples that separated her *datt's* farm from the Yoders', Emma thought about what she was going to

48

say to Samuel. A little part of her was nervous; would he understand her need to go to Ohio? A part of her knew she had to get this settled before she could even think about making any promises to him. She wasn't sure what he had on his mind, but one thing for sure and certain was he wanted to be more than friends.

Walking through the trees that bordered Yoders' strawberry fields, she saw Samuel near the edge watching his *datt*. Skillfully guiding a horse through the rows of barren plants, Levi sat on the back of a sickle mower cutting the old plants back. Walking up beside Samuel, they watched in unison as his *datt* mowed the field.

"I guess this isn't the year you need to plow them under and plant new?" Emma asked in a curious tone.

"No, not this year. We'll do that next summer."

Samuel looked at the blanket she had draped over her arm. "Were you down at the creek enjoying this fine summer day?" He leaned in and bumped her shoulder, whispering, "Had I known you were there I would have joined you. It would've been better than standing here watching my *datt* do all my work. He says handling a workhorse in the fields is a bit too much to put on my shoulder. All I know is I'm getting pretty sick and tired of standing around and watching everyone pick up my slack."

"But Samuel, you have to let your shoulder heal. I'm sure he doesn't want you to undo all the therapy you've already done. It's only been six weeks since you got hurt." Samuel noticed how caring her voice sounded.

"Even so, it makes for long days and restless nights," Samuel said. "A man needs to tire himself out with hard work if he expects to get a good night's sleep. Something I haven't had in quite a while now."

Emma patted his arm tenderly. "All in due time," she said soothingly. "Don't push yourself. By next strawberry season, you'll be good as new."

"Let's hope so."

Glancing down at the stack of letters tied with a pink ribbon, he asked, "What do you have there?"

"Letters from my birth mother."

49

"And how did that go?" He asked as he took his hat off and wiped his brow with the back of his hand.

"I learned a lot and decided I want to meet her."

"Is she coming here?"

"That's the problem. Daniel says she won't be able to leave Ohio and if I want to see her, I'll have to go to her. That's why I came over — to talk to you. I'm going to tell my parents that I'm going to Sugarcreek for a while. She gets out of prison next week, and I want to be there for her."

Samuel didn't say anything for a few minutes. He put his hat back on, looked at his feet, and kicked a stone around with the toe of his boot.

"For how long?"

"I'm not sure, it all depends."

"Depends on what?"

"On whether I can help her or not."

"What do you need to help her with?"

"Find *Gott* again."

Stooping to the ground to pick up a piece of used straw that was used as a mat between the rows, Samuel put it in his mouth.

"You do realize your mother isn't like a lost kitten that needs to be taken back to its momma. You can't force someone to turn to *Gott* if their heart isn't ready. I've read stories about prison. It's not pretty. Your mother may never be the person she once was, even if you don't know what she was like before."

Emma patted the letters in her hand and pointed to her *datt's* farm. "I've spent all afternoon reading over and over again the letters she wrote to me. She feels like *Gott* abandoned her. While she was sitting in a cell thinking the world had forgotten her, I was tucked safe and sound on this Amish farm. Little does my family know what she did for them."

"What are you talking about? As I see it, she gave you away without so much of a second thought to what would happen to you."

"You're not listening to me," Emma said in an aggravated tone.

Samuel stood back up. "I'm trying to follow you," he said, his manner questioning. "But you're talking in circles."

50

Emma took a deep breath. "Marie Cooper killed my father to save Jacob."

"What? How can you know that?"

"In her letters, she told me she had to make a choice. It was either stop my English father or let him kill the Amish man that laid on the ground in front of them. The only difference is she didn't know at the time that Jacob Byler would be the man who raised me."

Placing his hand on the small of her back, Samuel directed Emma to walk into the shade and out of the hot sun. "What I don't understand is how you think you can help her," he said. "What can you say or do that will make up for sixteen years of separation? I hope you don't think you can walk back into her life and everything be normal, do you?"

"No, of course not."

"You have to realize she has just spent time in prison with other criminals. She is going to be different than anyone you have ever come in contact with. I can't say I'm happy about that."

"I know, and neither are my parents going to be. But it's what I feel I need to do."

Looking over his shoulder to see where his *datt* was, Samuel took Emma's free hand in his and looked her in the eyes. "You know I will do anything to make you happy and if this is what you feel you need to do, then go. But promise me you'll write and stay in touch."

Taking a letter from the stack and removing the contents, she handed him the envelope.

"I think I'll stay with my Aunt Anna Mae if she has room. This is her address."

Folding it in half and tucking it in his back pocket, Samuel reached for her hand again and squeezed it. "I've waited this long to start courting you, a few more months isn't going to matter one way or another. Hurry back and be safe."

She squeezed his hand back. "I will," she said in a loving voice. "All I want to do is get to know her and help her see that *Gott* is still there if she'll look for Him."

Releasing her hand, Samuel's voice turned hopeful. "I'll pray that you can reach her and that you'll always want to call Willow Springs home."

Without saying a word, she turned and walk down the path that would lead her back to her parents' place and into a battle of wills that was sure to follow.

~~

Emma had been gone much longer than she had planned. Her *schwesters* were already peeling potatoes and snapping green beans for supper. It was only fitting Rebecca flew a snippy comment at her as soon as she entered the kitchen.

"We've been looking for you all afternoon. You could have told someone where you were going."

Even Anna, who typically didn't add to Rebecca's bossiness, nodded in agreement.

"You're right, I'm sorry," Emma said. "I should have let someone know where I was. I went down to the creek. What can I do to help with supper?"

"Nothing right now, we have it under control just like we've done all week." Rebecca shooed her away with a hand still holding tight to the potato peeler as she said. "*Mamm* was asking for you when she came downstairs. She's sitting in her chair in the other room."

Covering the letters with the blanket, Emma laid the bundle on the bottom step of the stairs and went into the living room. Pulling the bent-willow rocker closer and making sure the braided rug it sat on came with it, she sat on the edge of the seat and laid her hand on her *mamm's* knee.

"Are you feeling any better?"

"I am. Where did you run off to?"

"Just down to the creek. I wanted to be alone with my thoughts."

"And did it help?"

"I was able to sort a few things out. I'd like to talk to you and *Datt* after supper if you're up to it."

52

Before she could say another word, her *mamm* looked past her and into the kitchen. Turning in her chair, she saw her *datt* standing between the two rooms, gripping the straw hat he held in his hands, ready to scold.

"Where have you been? Your *schwesters* looked everywhere for you."

"I was down by the creek. I didn't mean to worry you. I thought I'd be back before anyone missed me. I stopped at the Yoders' on my way home. I'm sorry."

Jacob didn't move from his stance.

"I saw Daniel's truck parked beside Willow Creek Bridge on our way back from town," he said. "Would you know anything about that?"

Lowering her head long enough to decide how much she wanted to say, Emma looked at her *mamm* and then back to her *datt*.

"I do."

Reaching in her pocket to retrieve the phone, she held it up. "He gave me this last week and told me to call him when I was ready to talk. So, I called and ask him to meet me."

"You did what! I firmly told the both of you I didn't want you seeing each other."

Taking a few moments to choose her words carefully, she continued. "He's my *bruder*, and I have every right to see him."

"Not under this roof, you don't. I told Daniel, and I'll tell you again there is no reason why you need to spend time with each other. All he is going to do is cloud your judgment. It's only been a week since you found out about your birth mother. You need time to decide on your own accord how you want to proceed."

"But I've already figured that out."

"Figured what out?" Jacob's tone was stern.

"I want to go to Sugarcreek to meet her."

Hearing her *mamm* sigh, she turned to see pain etched on her already flushed face. Between the look on her *mamm's* face and reading the heart-wrenching words of failure in her birth mother's letters, Emma felt torn. How could she please them both? Jacob, on the other hand, didn't wait for her to finish. The sound of the screen door slamming and his heavy footsteps across the porch told her all she needed to know.

She would be going to Sugarcreek without their approval.

Chapter 6 - Sugarcreek

For the next few days Emma tried as best as she could to ease her *mamm's* worry about not returning to Willow Springs. Her *datt* refused to talk to her and avoided her at every turn. The disappointed expression carved on his forehead worried her. Trying to understand his need to protect her was the only thing that kept her from harboring ill feelings toward him.

Daniel stopped after his last delivery yesterday to tell her he had everything in place to leave first thing in the morning. His adoptive parents gave him their blessings and his boss approved an extended leave of absence.

Folding the last of her clothes and placing them neatly in the suitcase on her bed, Emma reached for the small wooden box. Opening it and adding its contents to her bag, she set the box aside. Closing the suitcase and setting in on the floor, she walked over to the window. Pulling the pleated curtain aside to allow the cool breeze to enter her room, she took a few minutes to look out over the farm she had called home for the last sixteen years. The smell of sawdust tickled her nose as thoughts of spending time with her *datt* in the furniture shop came to mind. The emptiness in the pit of her stomach brought tears to her eyes with the realization she was leaving without his blessing. *Would he ever forgive me for wanting to meet my birth mother?* Closing the window, she looked around the room one last time to be sure she hadn't forgotten anything before going to say her goodbyes.

Making her way down the stairs she set the suitcase by the front door, she went to the kitchen to sit with her *mamm* for a few minutes before Daniel was due to arrive.

"I hate to leave you when you still aren't feeling well. Is there anything I can get you?"

Stella smiled weakly. "Anna made me some tea before she left for the Flea Market and your *datt* will come in and check on me in a bit. I'll be fine."

Reaching in her pocket for the piece of paper she wrote her phone number on, Emma handed it to her *mamm*.

"I know you don't approve of the phone Daniel gave me, but I wanted to give you the number in case you need to reach me. I wrote to Aunt Anna Mae to tell her I was coming. If for some reason I can't stay with her or my plans change I will write and give you my address."

Stella placed the slip of paper in the bible she held on her lap and looked at her daughter.

"I know this is what you need to do, and I can't say I'm happy about you leaving, but *Gott* has a plan for you, and I pray it will lead you back home someday."

Emma took Stella's hands in her own. "I don't know what my future holds in Sugarcreek, but I have to go," she said, her voice loving. "I have to see if I can help her."

"I know dear, and I do understand. I really do."

"I wish *Datt* would."

"He will. Give him time."

Hearing Daniel's truck, Emma reached over, kissed her *mamm* on the cheek, and headed to the door. Daniel was waiting for her at the bottom of the stairs when she came outside.

"All ready?"

"As ready as I'll ever be. My stomach is in knots this morning, but I'm sure that has to do more with *Datt* than anything else."

"He still isn't talking to you?"

"No, he didn't even come in for breakfast this morning. Matthew tried to go outside and talk to him, but he won't budge. He feels I'm rushing things."

Daniel took her suitcase and put it in the bed of his pickup.

"Okay then, let's get started."

Walking around to the front of the truck, Emma stopped and waited for Matthew. He was walking from the shop. "No luck in convincing *Datt* to tell me bye?"

"The only one that's going to get him to soften up is *Mamm* and right now she doesn't have the energy to argue with him. Besides the Bishop is in there with him talking about who knows what."

"I'm worried about her."

"We'll worry about *Mamm*. You just go do what you need to do and get back here," Matthew said. "That's the only thing that's going to get this family back to normal."

Emma walked closer to give him a hug. "Thanks for being so understanding. You're the only one who's made this easy on me."

Matthew walked around Emma and reached out his hand to Daniel.

"And you. I'm counting on you to take care of our *schwester*." The friends shook hands.

"No worries here," Daniel replied. "You can count on it. Have you given any more thought to going back to Sugarcreek? I'm sure Nathan's offer to learn the horse business still stands. All you have to do is show up."

"I haven't had a chance to talk it over with *Datt* yet. I figured I'd wait until he got used to the idea of Emma being gone before I press it too much. I've thought of nothing else since he put the idea in my head about being a holding stable for him here in Willow Springs. I've spent the last two weeks cleaning and repairing the barn to meet his standards in case I can make it work. For sure and certain it's a good plan, but time will tell if that's what *Gott* wants me to do."

"If you change your mind, you know Nathan will welcome you, and Sarah will be glad to see you."

"Sarah. What am I missing? Emma asked, looking at Matthew.

Ignoring her question, Daniel motioned her to get in the truck and said.

"I'll fill you in on our drive if it's okay with your brother," Daniels said in a questioning voice.

"If you must. I'm sure she'll figure it out on her own when she sees Sarah's reaction when you show up without me." Matthew said as he turned to walk back to the barn.

Climbing up in the seat, Emma clicked her seatbelt and looked toward the shop hoping he would come out and say anything to her.

~~

Little did she know her *datt* stood in the shadows of the shop window saying a prayer for his youngest daughters' safe return. No matter how hard he tried, he couldn't help but be fearful of all she would discover in Sugarcreek. There was so much more he should have shared with her. In fact, so much more he should have shared with Stella, but didn't. Would his family ever forgive him?

Moving to the window with him, Bishop Weaver pulled on his long white beard as he said.

"You should have been the one to tell her."

"Maybe so. But I'd rather she be mad at me then break a promise. She'll find out soon enough that's for sure and certain."

~~

Looking in his rearview mirror to make sure the buggy he passed was far enough behind him, Daniel turned on to Troyer Lane and said. "We're here. Is your Aunt expecting you?"

"I sent her a letter. I hope she received it in time."

Pulling up in front of the small house, Daniel parked and sat still until Emma got up enough courage to open the door.

Wringing her hands on her lap, Emma said, "I don't know what I'm so nervous about?"

"Your Aunt is very sweet, and I'm sure she'll welcome you with open arms. Just be yourself, and everything will fall into place. Once I get your suitcase out, I'm going to Nathan's to make sure I have a place to stay and a job. I'll come back later this evening to check on you. Will you be okay?"

"I have to be. I have no other choice," Emma said as she pushed her door open.

Holding the suitcase in one hand, he reached over and pulled her into a side hug with the other and said.

"One day at a time. Today's obstacle is to settle in with Anna Mae. We have a few days before we need to go to Mayfield, so try to enjoy yourself. Do you want me to stay for a few minutes?"

Moving her head from side to side, she looked up when she heard the squeak of the screen door. Anna Mae greeted her with a warm smile, which made her instantly feel at ease.

"Emma, I've been watching the driveway for two days waiting for you." Anna Mae said as she held the door open for her to enter.

"Come inside out of the hot sun. I'll pour us all a glass of tea."

Carrying Emma's suitcase to the top of the stairs, Daniel said. "Not me, I need to go make sure I have a place to stay at the Bouterights', but I'll be back later to check on you both."

Turning toward Emma, he asked. "Do you need anything before I leave? You still have the phone in case you need me, right?"

Watching her Aunts reaction to his comment about the phone, she said. "I do, but I doubt I'll use it. I'm sure I'll be in good hands."

"She'll be fine. We have lots of catching up to do, and I'm sure she has questions for me. Now you get going to Nathan's. If you find you don't have a place to lay your head, you be sure to come back. My boy Martin has an extra bedroom in the house he hasn't filled with *kinner* yet. I'm sure it's yours if you need it." Anna Mae ushered Emma inside as they both waved goodbye to Daniel.

Standing just inside Anna Mae's door, Emma looked around the plain *doddi haus* which looked much like the one that sat unused at home.

"Martin setup an extra bed in my quilting room. You can take your suitcase in and make yourself at home. I'll go get us a snack and something to drink while you get settled."

Emma watched as her aunt retreated to the kitchen while she tried to adjust to her new surroundings. Making her way to the room her aunt pointed to, she stepped inside and smiled at the beautiful quilt top stretched out on the quilt frame near the window. The familiar Dahlia pattern in shades of blue and yellow made the room look bright and cheerful. It only took a few minutes to hang the dresses she brought and fill the drawers with stockings and undergarments. She left the contents of the box in the suitcase and pushed it under the bed out of the way. Making her way back down the short hallway and into the kitchen, she noticed her Aunt had everything laid on the table and was waiting for her to join her.

"All settled?" Anna Mae asked as she held out her hand, inviting her to sit across the table from her.

"I am. Thank you for allowing me to stay with you. I'm not sure how long though. Is that okay?"

"My *haus* is your *haus*. You stay for as long as you need. It feels good to have someone to take care of again."

Watching the smile spread across the short round woman's face, made Emma feel welcomed.

"Now tell me, how are your *Mamm* and *Datt*?"

"*Mamm* has been under the weather the last couple weeks, but she promised she'd go see the doctor next week if she wasn't any better. *Datt*, on the other hand, isn't talking to me. He wasn't too happy; I asked Daniel to bring me here." Her voice cracked slightly as she explained his reaction to her trip.

"I'm sure he's worried about you. I'll write to him and let him know you made it safely and reassure him I'll take good care of you."

Reaching across the small round oak table to pat Emma's hand, Anna Mae said.

"Now let's talk about why you're here."

Pulling away from the soft fingertips that lay on the back of her hand, she folded her hands in her lap before letting her know what her plans were. She was sure her reaction would be the same as her parents and braced herself for the lecture that was sure to follow. When she finished explaining what was in the letters and how she felt drawn to help her mother, she waited for her to respond. The only thing she left out was the fact that her father was Amish. The only people who knew were Daniel, herself and her birth mother. She needed more information about that fact before she shared it with anyone else.

Anna Mae took her time absorbing Emma's words before she commented.

"I have no idea what your mother may have gone through, but in a way, I feel responsible for her anguish. Every time I received

60

one of her letters, I prayed over it before I sent it on to your *datt*. Every year I felt the need to let her know you were safe. I knew it would come to this someday and I prayed she would understand I had to let that decision come from Jacob. I never understood why he was so adamant about not writing her, but again it wasn't my story to tell."

In a hopeful tone, Emma replied, "I don't understand either. Maybe someday he'll tell me. That is, if he ever starts talking to me again."

Reaching for a cookie from the plate that sat between them, Anna Mae broke a piece off and nibbled on it as she asked.

"Are you going to go see her?"

Emma took a long sip of the sweet minty tea her Aunt had poured for her before she answered.

"I won't need to. She wrote to Daniel to let him know she was being released on Monday. He'll go pick her up and bring her back to Sugarcreek. I haven't decided if I'll go with him yet. He's not sure he wants me to go. He said we would talk about it in a day or two. I told him I would let him decide."

Brushing cookie crumbs off the table and into her hand, Anna Mae thought for a few moments before she commented.

"I guess it's best you have some time to pray about it before Monday. *Gott* will tell you what he wants you to do. Just give it to Him and let Him handle it for you."

"*Gott* willing I'll see His hand in all of this and be able to help her find her way back to Him," Emma said as she stood to put her glass in the sink.

Tapping her fingers on the table as she watched her niece walk to the sink, Anna Mae waited until she turned back around before she continued.

"I hope you're not setting yourself up for more heartache. We have no idea of the condition of Marie's relationship with *Gott*. It may take more than some kind words from you to help her find her way back. How do we even know what kind of life she led before she killed her husband?"

Sitting back down in the chair opposite her aunt, Emma folded her fingers under her chin and leaned on her elbows. Looking past her aunt and out the screen door that led to the front porch, she said.

"You're right. I have no idea how she'll be when she gets here. All I know is she mentioned her mother made a point to give her a solid Christian upbringing before she met my father. I guess I'm hoping and praying I can still reach that part of her."

Nibbling on the other half of cookie she broke in half, Anna Mae asked.

"Has Daniel said if you have any other family in the area?"

"All he said was he didn't know anything about his father's family. Our mother was an only child as was her mother, so he didn't think so. When she went to prison, our grandmother was the only family he had to take care of him. When she died, he got placed in a foster home. I'm not sure if they looked for any other family to take him in. He has a lot of hurt feelings himself to work through. As I have some of my own with *Mamm* and *Datt* keeping this from me for so long."

Taking a deep breath and blowing it out to make a sigh, Emma asked.

"Do you remember hearing or reading anything about my mother that might help? I can only imagine a murder in an Amish community would make the news. The more I know about her past and what she might have gone through with my father might help me reach her."

Pondering Emma's question, Anna Mae tried to think back to that week so many years ago.

"That was a long time ago, and it was a confusing week. My *Datts'* funeral was that week, and there were people in and out of the house for days. Stella's baby girl died, Jacob was nursing his injuries, and of course, we had you. We still had no idea what we were going to do with you or if or when someone would come for you. If I remember correctly, Jacob and your Uncle Walter spent a good bit of time with Bishop Shetler that week. I'm not sure what they discussed, but you may want to start with him. If the police wanted to talk to any of us, they would have started with the Bishop first. I remember thinking it was strange no one ever came."

'Is he still the Bishop of this district?"

"He is. He lives just over the ridge a couple of miles. Church is at his house this week. I can introduce you to him if you'd like on Sunday."

"Yes, of course."

Standing to put the plate of cookies back in the tin on the counter, Anna Mae said.

"How about I go introduce you to your cousins. I'm sure they're dying to figure out who's visiting their *Mommi*.

Chapter 7 - Sarah and Nathan

Sarah stood at the kitchen sink washing dishes hoping the afternoon mail would bring word from Matthew. It had been two weeks since he left with Daniel to go back to Willow Springs. He left in such a hurry she knew it had to be something important for him to leave after promising her he'd stay. After being away from each other for over a year, this recent time apart had been the hardest. Her thoughts were consumed with him and the plans they'd made. Her hopes and desires all died the day her *schwester* Susan died in a buggy accident. Nathan, her brother-in-law, was in no hurry to find a new *fraa* and *mamm* for Rachel and Amos. Looking back, she wished she would have told her father about Matthew before she left. Had she been honest with him, he may not have pushed her to stay so long in Sugarcreek. In the back of her mind, she knew her family was hoping she'd marry Nathan. That would never happen; her heart belonged to Matthew.

Hearing the familiar sound of tires on the gravel driveway, Sarah looked out the window curious to see who may be visiting. Most likely, it would be one of Nathan's customers coming to look over his horses. Nathan built up his stables so much, customers traveled across the country to purchase his highly trained buggy horses. Offering Matthew, a chance to run a holding stable in Willow Springs was another way he could reach his customers in Northwestern Pennsylvania. She prayed Matthew would accept his offer and come stay with them so he could learn from Nathan. Recognizing Daniels truck, Sarah quickly wiped her hands and headed to the front porch. Disappointed that Matthew wasn't with him, she put a big smile on her face anyways.

"Daniel, welcome. What brings you back to Sugarcreek so soon?"

"I'm hoping I can talk Nathan into giving me a place to sleep in exchange for work at the stables for a short while. Is he anywhere around?"

"He was just in for dinner. He took Rachel and Amos for a walk to the barn while I cleaned up the kitchen. He won't be long. Come sit while you wait on him."

Sitting in the willow rocker closest to the door, Sarah pointed to the chair beside her, inviting him to join her.

"For sure and certain, Nathan will be more than happy to have you. He's still short a couple of stable hands. Will you be sticking around this time?"

"It all depends on Emma."

"Emma?" Sarah said in a surprised tone. "Matthew's sister?"

"It's a long story. Here comes Nathan now. I'll explain it to both of you at the same time."

Sarah loved watching Nathan with his *kinner*. He took the time to answer every question they had, even if Amos asked the same question four or five times in a row. Rachel would be starting school this year, and Amos, even at four years old, had a sweet and caring heart -- just like his *mamm* did. They all still missed Susan, but they were starting to get back on the road to a normal life again. Amos had started to call her *mamm* a few months ago, and neither of them had the heart to correct him. At some point, she was going to have to go back to her life in Willow Springs with Matthew. She knew it was time to start convincing Nathan to start looking for a *fraa*.

Directing Rachel and Amos to go play, Nathan headed up the stairs as he said.

"Missing Rosie's apple pie already?"

"I sure am," as he stood to extend his hand to Nathan.

"What has you back so soon? I hope you and Matthew got everything taken care of at home. You both took off so quickly we didn't know what to think."

"Sorry about that. I'll explain it all to you in a minute. I'm sticking around for a while this time, and Sarah tells me you're still short a couple hands. Will mine do?"

65

Leaning back on the porch railing, Nathan said. "I can put you to work, that's for sure."

For the next thirty minutes, Daniel went into the long story about his mother and finding his sister. The only thing he didn't divulge was the fact that his biological father was Amish, Emma had asked him not to. He even went as far as explaining how their neighbor, Anna Mae Troyer fit into it all.

Playing with the strings of her *kapp*, Sarah listened intently to the story Daniel was telling. Now she understood why Matthew had to leave so quickly and why he didn't return with Daniel.

"How is Emma doing?" Sarah asked.

"She's been a trooper. She's handled it pretty well-considering everything she's gone through. When I dropped her off at Anna Mae's, she was a little nervous, but her Aunt seemed to calm her quickly."

"I'm sure she did," Sarah said. "Anna Mae is the sweetest woman I know, and Emma is in good hands."

Nathan pushed himself up to sit on the railing and asked. "So, what now?"

"On Monday, I'll pick her up from the woman's prison in Mayfield. From there, I'm not sure. I haven't figured out what I'm going to do with her yet. I bought a newspaper at the gas station when I got into town. I'm hoping I can find her an apartment today."

Nathan stood and stretched his back as he said.

"Sounds like you'll have your hands full. Take care of finding your mother a place to live, and once you have everything in order, I'll put you to work. For now, I have a business to run, and nothing is getting done with me sitting here. You know what time supper is, and as always Sarah makes plenty."

Turning his attention back to Sarah, he asked. "How is my *Mamm*?"

"About the same. I was able to get her up and into the sitting room after dinner, but her hands and feet are hurting something awful. The rain last night hasn't helped her arthritis none. I made her a cup of ginseng tea, gave her a book, and found her reading glasses. She said she was going to sit in her chair the rest of the day."

Taking the steps two at a time, Nathan hollered over his shoulder as he headed back to the barn. "I hope you brought your muscles. I have two hundred fence posts coming next week."

Standing to holler back, Daniel said. "On second thought, maybe I'll find another place to sleep!"

"Too late. A deal is a deal, and we already shook on it."

Turning back to Sarah, Daniel laughed and said. "I hope I can keep up with him. It's been a long time since I did any hard labor."

Reaching in his back pocket, he retrieved a letter from Matthew and handed it to her and said.

"I need to go check out a few apartments. I'll be back around supper. Is there anything you need in town?"

"No, I don't think so. Thanks for not giving me this when Nathan was around. I've not explained to him about Matthew yet."

"No problem. Matthew told me to give it to you in private."

Sarah waited until Daniel had left before she gave herself permission to open Matthew's letter.

Sarah,

I'm sorry I was not able to come back to Sugarcreek with Daniel. By now, he has explained everything to you. I have not talked to Datt about Nathan's offer. I plan to do so soon. Mamm has not been feeling well, and he has had a lot on his mind. It has been hard for me to find the right time. I'm praying he will be open to Nathan's offer. Even though Datt has the Furniture Shop, this is still his farm, and I need to discuss it with him. I plan to talk to him soon. In the meantime, I'm praying that you find the right time to tell Nathan about us. It wouldn't be fair for him not to know of our plans.

I spent some time looking around the farm for the perfect spot to build our haus. If I extend the driveway past the barn and into the back field, we will have a perfect view of the Sugar Maple trees that line the property. In the fall they will give us a wonderful color show. To the left of the house will make a great spot for your kitchen garden and ample room for kinner to play. I'm looking forward to making you my fraa and building our life together. Gott willing, everything will work out in our favor. I will work on my datt, and you work on getting Nathan to find a suitable fraa so you can come back to Willow Springs. Gott has a plan, we just have to wait for it. Sometimes waiting on Gott to show us the way is harder than believing He has a purpose for everything He does. I am praying for patience and wisdom to not open any doors He may not be ready for us to walk through yet.

Until I see you again,
All my love Matthew

Taking a few minutes to imagine what their new *haus* may look like, her heart swelled with a longing to be in Matthew's arms. Reading how he was putting it in *Gotts'* hand reassured her that he was the man for her. A *mun* who would be led by the Lord would lead their family well. She had to believe, as he did, that *Gott* had a plan and He would work it all out in His own time, not theirs.

Timing it perfectly, Rachel and Amos ran up the stairs and required Sarah's attention. For one thing for sure, she needed to fill Nathan in on Matthew. She couldn't chance another conversation like last night without him knowing her true intentions. It wouldn't be fair.

Sarah kept busy the rest of the day tending to the *kinner* and keeping Nathan's *mamm* comfortable. Over the last year, Rosie's health had declined. Her arthritis kept her from helping with the *kinner* and tending to the *haus* like she had done before she'd arrived. It was like she had three children to care for not just two. But she didn't mind, that was what *Gott* had sent her to Sugarcreek to do anyways.

More than once throughout the day, Sarah wondered what Nathan was so anxious to talk to her about. Last night he convinced her to sit on the porch with him. Not wanting to hurt his feelings, and putting it in such a way she couldn't say no. She sat down in the rocker beside him.

It was the first time she took a good look at him. The flecks of silver that edged the hair around his temples reminded her of their twenty-year age difference. Studying the serious look on his face, she was reminded of how many times over the last couple of weeks she'd caught him looking at her more intently than he ever had before. She wasn't oblivious to the way he watched her and how he went out of his way to check on her throughout the day. So much so, it started to make her uncomfortable.

Thinking back to their conversation last night, she thanked *Gott* for Rachel's perfect timing in interrupting them. Her long braid and cotton nightgown trailed after her as she came barreling out the door and climbed up in her lap crying about a nightmare.

Picking her up without looking back at Nathan, she led her away and back up the stairs to her room. Dodging the uncomfortable conversation one more time she curled up in bed with her niece and fell asleep beside her. By the time she woke up and walked to her own house across the yard, Nathan was long gone from the porch.

~~

Trying to concentrate on the feed invoices on his desk, Nathan played over in his head the conversation he tried to have with Sarah the night before.

Thinking back to how she looked when she came outside made him smile. The soft glow from the oil lamp that hung over the kitchen table made a halo effect behind her starch white *kapp*. When she turned to catch the door so it wouldn't slam and wake the children, the light added specks of color to her Chicory colored eyes. In the past, whenever he saw the blue wildflowers growing in ditches throughout Holmes County he thought of Suzy. But lately, they reminded him of Sarah. When she handed him his coffee their fingers touched for only a brief second, but it was long enough to feel the warmth of her hand. He missed the softness of Suzy's skin. He couldn't help but wonder if Sarah would feel the same. He knew he shouldn't be having these thoughts about his sister-in-law, but her closeness was clouding his judgement.

Thinking back to how close he had gotten to sharing his thoughts with her, he wondered if she was feeling the same way.

Taking the cup, she handed him he asked.

"Where's yours?"

Moving toward the steps, Sarah said.

"I'm going on to bed. The *kinner* wore me out today." Catching her by the arm, he pulled her back and said. "Oh no you don't, I look forward to our time together without the *kinner* pulling you away. Come sit with me for a few minutes you haven't stopped all day."

Giving in to his plea, she took a seat next to him.

Pulling on his beard and shifting in his seat, he said. "I've wanted to talk to you about something."

"What's that?"

Clearing his throat, he said." You know Suzy's been gone from us for more than a year now."

Crossing her arms and rubbing them to generate some heat, she said. "I know. I miss her every day."

Taking a sip of his coffee, he continued.

"You're good for the *kinner*, and they love you as much as they did their *mamm*."

Smiling and pushing her foot to rock the chair, she said.

"I love them too. I see Susan in them more and more each day. Rachel looks so much like her when she was her age it's uncanny. And that Amos is growing up to look just like you. If he doesn't stop growing, he'll pass you by in no time."

Kicking his legs out in front of him, he said. "I'm sure he has a lot more to do to catch up with these long legs.

They both smiled at his comment and sat in silence for a few minutes before Rachel came out on the porch crying about a nightmare.

Shaking the memory from his head, he tried again to concentrate on the stack of invoices in front of him. He looked forward to their time on the porch, long after the *kinner* had gone to bed and his *Mamm* had turned in for the day. It was the same evening routine Suzy, and he had shared. He didn't think he would ever get over the pain of losing her, but with Sarah's help, he felt like life was worth living again.

He noticed Sarah hadn't been herself the last couple of weeks, but he couldn't pinpoint what the problem was. She was distracted and often came up with excuses why she couldn't sit with him. She reminded him of Suzy. Their mannerisms were the same, they sounded the same, looked identical and other than their age difference they could have been twins. When she was around, he missed Suzy a little less. More often than not, he found himself wondering if maybe *Gott* put her in his path to fill Suzy's shoes. Could he be falling in love with her? Or was her familiarity clouding his judgment? All he knew was Rachel and Amos loved her, and she filled the hole left behind by Suzy's death.

He wasn't sure he loved her the way he loved Suzy, but at this point, all he knew was he liked the way she made him feel when she was near. That was at least a good start. He vowed he would try again to talk to her. As he saw it, it only made sense. Why else would *Gott* send her unless to help him?

Putting the papers in a folder on his desk and pushing them aside to call it a day. He heard Daniels voice as he joked around with a few of the stable hands outside. He left the office to join them.

Slapping Daniels back on his way past he asked. "Did you find an apartment for your mother today?'

"No not yet, but I still have a couple days. It seems most people know her name and aren't too fond of renting to a convict without a job."

Nathan stopped to rub the nose of one of the Standardbred's that had just been delivered before he offered his advice.

"Sugarcreek is a small town, news travels as fast as it does through the Amish grapevine. Keep at it, and I bet you'll find someone who'll give her a chance."

'I hope so, or she'll be sleeping in my truck."

"Sarah is sure to have supper about ready. Are you going to join us?"

"Sounds good, I didn't stop for lunch today. I'm starving."

Following Nathan through the stables and back into the house, Daniel was greeted to the wonderful smells of supper the minute he walked in the door.

Stopping to take his boots off, he heard Rosie call his name before he made it to the table.

"Daniel Miller, I swear you smell apple pie all the way from Pennsylvania. That's twice we've had your favorite dessert on the table, and you found your way back to join us."

Walking over to her, he patted her shoulder and said how nice it was to see her. Falling into his regular spot at Nathan's table, he waited for the other stable hands to follow suit. Nathan treated all of his regular live-in workers' like family and each were invited to share meals with him.

After everyone had filled their plates and bowed their heads, Sarah asked Daniel if he had any luck finding a place for his mother to live.

"Not yet, but I'm not giving up."

Without thinking about what Nathan might say, she said.

"I have an extra bed in my room. She can stay with me until you figure something out."

Daniel was buttering a slice of bread and didn't notice Nathan stop his fork in mid-air to glare at Sarah's offer.

Feeling Nathan's eyes on her, she raised her eyebrows as if to ask what the problem was. He didn't have to say a word for her to know he wasn't happy she had offered his home to Daniel's mother.

Taking a bite of the warm bread, Daniel licked the dripping butter off the side and looked toward Sarah and back at Nathan.

"If you're sure it wouldn't be too much trouble? It would help until she gets a job and a place of her own."

Taking a few seconds to answer, Nathan used the extra time to thoroughly chew the bite he had placed in his mouth, giving himself enough time to contemplate what he was being asked to approve. Even though he wanted to help Daniel, he wasn't sure he wanted Marie Cooper living anywhere near his children or in the same house as Sarah. He couldn't help but think Suzy would have never allowed such a thing. How could Sarah put him on the spot like this without even consulting him first?

"I'll think about it," was all he said before he went back to cleaning his plate.

Sarah didn't have to look at Nathan to know she had overstepped her bounds with him. She had seen that look on his face before and knew it well. She may look like her *schwester* Susan, but that was as far as it went. Her mouth often got her in trouble more times than not. Her *schwester* was good at knowing her place and kept her thoughts to herself like a good Amish woman was taught to do. She on the other hand, failed to learn that yet.

Chapter 8 - Church Sunday

Emma sat on the porch listening to the chirping of a squirrel in a nearby tree as she waited for Anna Mae to get ready for church. In the five days since she had arrived in Sugarcreek, she had quickly fallen into the routines of the Troyer household. Her little cousins came over every morning to check on her, and she was enjoying helping her cousin Martin in his Greenhouse. Daniel had been over a few times to check on her, and Anna Mae was thrilled to have company. The only uneasiness she had was listening to Daniel's concern about where their mother would stay. Nathan hadn't given him an answer yet. But did say he wanted to talk to the Bishop first.

Anna Mae came out of the house at the same time Martin pulled his black-top family buggy in front of the *doddi haus*. Helping her Aunt in the buggy and taking a seat in the back, she picked up Martin's youngest *kinner* and placed her on her lap. Reaching up to slide the small window open to let the morning breeze in, Emma put her other arm around the little blonde-haired girl to keep her from sliding off her lap. Her mind was already contemplating what she was going to ask Bishop Shetler if she found the opportunity to speak to him. She prayed he would remember something about her mother or know if her Amish father had family in the area.

~~

Hurrying the *kinner* through breakfast and hoping they wouldn't soil their church clothes, Sarah spent the morning tiptoeing around Nathans sour mood. The closer they got to Monday, the more he punished her with his silent treatment for offering shelter to Daniel's mother. He had yet to give Daniel his answer but made it clear he wasn't pleased with her. Even though she didn't like the thoughts of him being upset with her, it did keep them off the porch and away from his uncomfortable conversations. Maybe after her little episode, he had changed his mind and would stop hinting of courtship. All she knew, she was doing everything she could to stay out of his way.

Wiping up the milk Amos had spilled on the table, Sarah look toward Rachel and said.

"Finish up, your *datt* will be pulling the buggy up any minute. We don't want to keep him waiting."

Pouring another cup of coffee for Rosie and carrying it to the front room, she set it down on the table beside her.

"Can you think of anything else you might need while we are gone? Nathan won't want to leave you home alone too long, so I'm sure we will come home right after the service."

"No dear, I think you have me settled in quite nicely. Now go tend to the *kinner* and stop fussing over me. I'll be fine."

Rosie was sharp as a tack, but when her Rheumatoid Arthritis flared up, her hands and feet took the worse of it, especially when it came to walking or standing. She hated not taking her to church but getting her in and out of the buggy during one of her flareups was close to impossible.

Lightly patting her swollen knuckles, Sarah said.

"When I get back, I'll rub more of that cream on them the doctor gave you."

Shooing her away, she took both hands and cautiously wrapped them around the mug Sarah had left beside her.

~~

Pulling the buggy up close to the house to wait for Sarah and the *kinner*, Nathan watched as Daniel and the other stable hands hooked the open wagon up to one of the horses they had been working with. He wanted to help Daniel out, but he wasn't going to give him an answer until he had a chance to speak with the Bishop. It was one thing to be a good neighbor and help those in need, but an English woman and one that had killed her husband. He wasn't sure about that. Only the Bishop could help him decide.

~~

Pulling his baseball cap down to shield the sun, Daniel climbed up in the wagon and lightly slapped the reins to put the horse in motion. Tipping his head in Nathan's direction as he passed, he hoped his friend would agree to let his mother stay with Sarah.

Feeling at home in the familiar surroundings, he was looking forward to seeing some of his Amish friends at worship. It wasn't the first time he'd attended the three-hour service. Amish or not, if you worked at the stables, you were expected to be there. His faded blue jeans, baseball cap, and cowboy boots made him stick out like a sore thumb, but this community welcomed him all the same. He prayed they would do the same for his mother. He wasn't sure why he felt such a connection to this community but couldn't help but think it might have something to do with his biological father being Amish. Someday he hoped he'd find out more about that tidbit of information Emma and he had just discovered.

The two-mile ride to Bishop Shetler's home went by quickly, and he soon found himself unhitching the wagon and tethering his horse to the long line that had been secured in the middle of the field. Following the other stable hands to the barn where the men gathered, he looked out over the women that stood in line waiting to go inside looking for Emma. Her dark blue dress and heavy brown bonnet stood out as much as his English clothes did. Hoping she felt at ease, he'd check on her after the service and before they spoke to Bishop Shetler.

~~

Taking a seat near the back of the room beside the other single women, Sarah got Rachel settled just as the Ministers and Bishop entered the room. Each woman was greeted with a handshake before they left to decide who was preaching the first sermon. The men started to file in as she watched for Nathan. The air in the Bouteright home had been as thick as a winter storm that morning, and she prayed Nathan would get some reassurance and peace during the day's message. With an edge in his voice, he took Amos from her once they got out of the buggy and told her he would be sitting with him. Watching as he guided the toddler to the seat beside him he didn't look over and acknowledge her as he usually did. A part of her was relieved, and her desire to go home to Matthew got stronger and stronger with each passing day. Giving her the silent treatment only reinforced the need for him to find a suitable *fraa* and *mamm* to the *kinner*. He had to realize, she wasn't Suzy and never would be.

~~~

Finding it easy to fall into place with helping with the fellowship meal, Emma followed Anna Mae to the kitchen to start serving the men. Anna Mae took the time to properly introduce her to her friends and put her to work, filling the water glasses that had already been placed on the tables. Starting with the Bishop, Emma politely reached in front of him to retrieve his glass. He was in an in-depth conversation with the towering man to his left. She hadn't meant to eavesdrop but when she heard Daniel's name she couldn't help but listen. Assuming the man was Nathan Bouteright, she was intrigued at why he would want to speak to the Bishop about her *bruder*. Nathan stopped when he noticed her and said.

"This is Emma, Daniel Millers *schwester* from Willow Springs. She is staying with Anna Mae Troyer whiles she is here."

Emma, startled that Nathan introduced her without being adequately introduced themselves continued to fill his glass and said.

"Bishop, it's nice to meet you."

Looking to Nathan, she said. "Nathan, I assume?"

"That it is. Are you enjoying your stay with Anna Mae?"

"I am. It's nice to get to know my family here."

Setting his glass down, she looked toward the Bishop and asked.

"If you're not too busy after the meal, could I ask you a few questions?

Picking up a slice of bread and adding a spoonful of peanut butter spread to it, he said.

"It seems everyone requires counsel from me this morning. Daniel caught me outside and already informed me the two of you wish to speak with me. Nathan has requested the same. I can only assume it has to do with Marie Cooper."

In a surprise, but confused voice, they both said in unison.

"You know her?"

"I know of her, but I wouldn't say I know her. We can speak later. For now, let us finish our meal."

Without questioning him further, she went about filling glasses hoping to see Daniel in the crowd and let him know the Bishop already knew of their mother. For the next hour she repeated the same process until all had eaten.

After she helped the women put the kitchen back in order, she walked outside to look for Daniel. To her surprise, he was standing near the corner of the barn with Nathan and the Bishop. Walking toward them, but staying her distance until she was sure she would be welcomed into their conversation, she saw Daniel gently shake his head no in her direction. She took that as a clue not to interrupt them. Turning to walk in the opposite direction, she saw Sarah coming her way.

"Emma, I'm sorry I've not gotten over to your Aunt's to say hello. Nathan's *mamm* has been under the weather, and I've had my hands full with the *kinner*."

"Oh my, don't think twice about it. I'd already planned to walk over and visit with you today." Emma said as she stooped down to talk to the *kinner* that flanked Sarah's side.

"And who do we have here. We've not formally been introduced."

Rachel spoke up first. "I'm Rachael, and this is my *bruder*, Amos."

Extending her hand to properly meet them, Emma said.

"It's so nice to meet you, Rachel and *bruder* Amos."

Standing up, she looked toward the three men standing in the shadow of the barn.

"I wanted to talk to the Bishop this morning, but it looks like Nathan and Daniel have him occupied. I can only imagine they're talking about Marie staying with you."

"I'm sure of it. Nathan was not too happy; I suggested she stay with me. It would be silly for her to worry about getting a place of her own so soon when I have plenty of room in the *doddi haus*."

"I can't thank you enough for suggesting it. Hopefully, the Bishop will approve it. I know Daniel is concerned he couldn't find her a place in town."

Sarah laid her hand on Emma's arm. "How are you doing?" she asked. "This had to have been a shock for you."

"It was. I still feel like it's a bad dream, but each day gets a little easier. Tomorrow is going to be difficult for all of us."

Looking back over toward the men, Emma watched as they all still huddled in a circle. Nathan was spinning his hat in his hands; Daniel stood with his hands in his pockets listening intently to the Bishop. She wished she could hear what was being discussed.

~~

Letting Nathan voice his concern about allowing Daniel's mother to be around his *kinner*, the Bishop tried to weigh each word carefully. Daniel was no stranger to his *g'may* and he considered him a part of the community. Nathan, however, was a respected member. He wanted to take his apprehension into consideration.

Crossing his arms in front of him, thumb under his chin, the Bishop spoke in an authoritative voice. "I see no harm in letting her stay with Sarah for the time being. As I see it, Sarah has her hands full and could use an extra set of hands. It can't be easy tending to your *kinner*, *mamm* and all of those stable hands. This community counts on the support your stable provides, and it wouldn't be well to have any of you overworked. As I see it, *Gott's* word tells us he doesn't show favoritism — and that means he loves Marie Cooper as much as he loves Nathan Bouteright."

The Bishop put his hands in his pockets and looked at Daniel. "I spent much time with Walter Troyer and Jacob Byler the weeks following your mother's arrest. I know the situation well and have prayed for her, you and your sister on many occasions."

Daniel looked confused. "You've known who my mother was all along?"

Nathan was surprised by the Bishop's answer. "Then you know she was sent to prison for killing my father."

"I do," the Bishop replied. "I also know if she didn't stop him, he would have killed Jacob Byler."

The looks on their faces told him he had said enough for now. He didn't need to let Nathan or Daniel know just how much he knew about Marie Cooper and the life she lived before the Mayfield Women's Prison.

The Bishop directed his next few words to Nathan. "*Gott* doesn't instruct us to just listen to His word, He expects us to do what it says."

Leaving them both to ponder his words, he turned to walk away. Across the yard stood Emma. The coloring of her hair and the familiar shape of her face reminded him of a pain he had buried a long time ago. It was the same twinge of anguish he felt every time he laid eyes on Daniel Miller. He wished he could avoid the whole wretched entanglement, but there she was, poor girl. She deserved to have her questions answered too.

"Bishop Shetler, do you have a few minutes I can speak to you?" Emma was polite; thank Jacob and Stella for that, the Bishop thought.

"Certainly, what can I help you with today?"

Looking over to Daniel and hoping he would join her, Emma noticed he was still talking with Nathan.

"I was hoping to speak with you. I'm sure Nathan and Daniel have filled you in about Marie Cooper. I hear you were the Bishop when she gave me to Walter. My aunt told me I should ask you if you remember anything about her that might help me. Anna Mae said if anyone would know or remember it would be you."

"That was a long time ago. However, I have to tell you it was me who suggested you go to Willow Springs. We had no idea what was going to happen with your mother, and you needed a home. No

80

one ever came to ask about you, and for that matter, I'm not sure the police even knew you existed."

Trying to make sense of how they wouldn't know about her, Emma shook her head. "Do you ever remember reading if my biological father had family in the area?"

Taking a few moments to answer, the Bishop could honestly say he didn't. "I don't remember reading about his family."

Not wanting to cut her short, but anxious to leave the discussion, he excused himself. "I know I wasn't much help, but please know if there is anything else I can do my door is always open."

Standing in the middle of the yard, no closer to knowing anything about Marie or her father, Emma shook her head and mumbled out loud. "Oh help, that was useless."

Looking around for Daniel, she spotted him walking her way. "So how did it go with Nathan?" she asked as he got closer.

"He has agreed to let her stay with Sarah, but he's not happy about it. The Bishop gave his permission, but he's still reluctant. I can't say I blame him any. I'm not sure I'd want my kids around a woman who'd been in prison either. I'm not sure I want to be around her myself."

"Daniel, she's our mother. How can you say that?"

"I know. Forgiveness, right?" Daniel was surprised at his reaction as well as Emma's. "I just hate not knowing the whole story. I get bits and pieces, but nothing makes sense. I have a feeling the Bishop knows more than he's letting on. Why would he agree so easily to let a stranger, an outsider at that, to stay in his *g'may*?"

Emma elbowed him. "He wouldn't lie to us, he's the Bishop."

"I didn't say he lied to us, but I'm not sure he's telling us everything he knows either. And for the record, you're too gullible."

Emma laughed. "Rightly so, I guess. You have to remember I've led a sheltered life and aren't as worldly as you." She elbowed him again.

"It's good to see you smile again. Hold onto it a bit longer. You may need it tomorrow when you meet our mother."

Her expression became serious. "Then you decided I should go with you?"

"It's up to you. I think it would be good if the three of us spent some time together alone. I have to pick her up at ten o'clock so I'll need to leave by eight if you want to go."

She already knew the answer. "Yes, I do."

Chapter 9 - Meeting Marie

After checking in with the guard at the gate, Daniel parked his truck in the lot he was directed to and turned toward Emma. Hands folded tightly in her lap, she looked ready to cry. He watched her take in the surroundings. The barbed wire-lined walls and the armed guard had to be overwhelming.

"We don't need to go any further than this, and you can stay put if you want," he assured her. "I'm going to get out and stretch my legs."

Emma rolled down the window to get some fresh air. "Good," she replied, "because I don't think I could move if I wanted to."

Leaving Emma in the truck, Daniel needed to gather his thoughts before he laid eyes on the woman he had pushed out of his mind for so long. Leaning back on the hood, he crossed his arms as if putting up a protected barrier from the emotions men weren't supposed to show. The conversation his adoptive father had with him before he left home played in his head.

"Son, no matter how hard you deny it, your mother and sister are going to need you. The ties that bind you as a family will never go away. You need to dig deep into the way you've been raised and be a pillar of strength they can lean on. This is going to be a whole new world for Emma, and you'll need to protect her from it. As for your mother, I have a feeling she'll have baggage of her own. As men and leaders of our family, there are times in life when we put our own needs aside and take care of those God has entrusted us with. Lean in on the Lord, and He'll show you the path he wants you to take."

All morning his adoptive father's words rang over and over in his mind. No one but the Lord could protect them and fix this broken family. Closing his eyes and saying a little prayer, he asked God for the strength his father spoke about.

When he opened his eyes, he saw her. There was no denying the woman in baggy clothes was his mother. The slim figure staring back at him was a female version of himself. The only picture he had seen of her in the last sixteen years was her booking photo. He wasn't sure what he expected, but he didn't imagine she'd look so much like him. Dropping his hands, he stood taller, trying to brace himself for the unknown.

~~

Standing outside the door that kept her from her family for so long, Marie took a deep breath and stepped off the curb and into her new life. Forcing herself to put one foot in front of the other was all she could do. Walking toward the man, not the little boy she remembered, was the hardest thing she had to face. As she got closer, she saw the faint shadow of someone else in the truck, but at that moment all she could do was look into Daniel's eyes, hoping for any sign of compassion. For a split second, the joy she felt in seeing him made her want to wrap her arms around him. But the thoughts of letting another person touch her, even a hug from a child, was more than she could handle. The bruises she endured for five years left a lifetime of emotional scars she wasn't sure anyone could break through. No, she couldn't or wouldn't let the feel of another person's touch break down those walls. There were no words to begin to make up for the pain she saw in his eyes. Part of her wanted to run back inside. At least there she wouldn't have to see the pain in his face. This was going to be a lot harder than she thought.

"Thank you." Marie's voice was quiet, almost apologetic.

"No problem" was all he said. He didn't move from his stance.

Seeing the movement behind him, Marie watched a young girl open the door and walk around the front of the truck. Confused by the dark dress and prayer *kapp*, a small gasp escaped her lips as her eyes landed on her face. Looking back at her was an image of her late husband, Jake. It was the eyes, the shape of the nose and high cheekbones that gave it away. There was no mistaking it. It was Elizabeth.

Looking back at Daniel and then again at the girl, she asked in a cracking voice. "Elizabeth?"

"Emma, Emma Byler," the girl said as she took a step closer. Out of instinct, Marie backed up like a wounded animal, not letting the girl get any closer.

"Oh, I'm sorry I thought you were …"

The girl cut her off before she could finish her sentence. "I'm Elizabeth, but I'd prefer you call me Emma."

Marie looked at Daniel. "You found her. Why didn't you tell me?"

"It happened so fast I didn't have time to let you know. But we can tell you all about it on our way back to Sugarcreek."

"Sugarcreek? But I have an appointment with my parole officer tomorrow morning in Mayfield."

"It will be fine. I'll bring you back for your appointment. Let's tackle one thing at a time. Right now let's get you out of here and home."

"Where's home?"

"For now you'll be staying at the Bouteright Stables with me until we find you a place of your own."

It was all too much. Marie stood frozen to the ground looking at her children, not knowing what to do next. Behind bars her days were planned to the very minute and she knew what to expect from day to day. Here, in the middle of a parking lot, watching her children stare back at her, she didn't know what to do or for that matter what to say. Daniel had grown into a man and Elizabeth was someone she didn't know. She wanted to cry, but those tears had dried the day she handed Elizabeth over to a stranger.

The uncomfortable silence between them felt like time standing still. It was Daniel who broke the spell. "This is going to be difficult for all of us, but let's try to make the best of it." With that, he opened the driver's side door for them both and motioned them to get in.

Marie stood, looking at the bench seat. Her heart raced at the thought of being trapped in the middle. "I'd rather sit by the door if that's okay?"

Emma spoke up. "That's fine. I'll sit in the middle."

After watching Emma slip in and look for the seat belt, Marie walked around to the passenger side and climbed in. After clicking herself in place, she moved as close to the door as possible.

Crossing her arms tight to her chest, Marie tried not to stare at the girl who sat beside her. Looking down at the girl's feet, she took note of her black, non-stylish rubber-soled shoes and black stockings. From what she remembered, the Amish in Sugarcreek often wore flip flops in the summer, and the style of *kapp* she wore was unlike those she saw while waiting tables at Sugar Valley.

Marie wanted to know more about the girl who inherited the looks of her late husband. "Emma, are you from Ohio?"

"No, Pennsylvania. Willow Springs to be exact."

Marie looked around her at Daniel. "Willow Springs?"

"Yes, the one and only," Emma said. "He and my brother are friends, and we've known each other for some time now."

Shaking her head, Marie tried to comprehend what she heard. "But how? How did you end up there?"

For the next eighty-seven miles, Daniel filled her in on how they found each other and what turmoil it had caused Emma's family. By the time he finished, they had turned into the driveway and pulled to a stop at the white picket fence that led to Bouteright Stables.

Daniel looked at Emma. "Do you want me to take you back to your aunt's house or do you want to come with us to Nathan's?"

Sounding surprised, Marie asked, "Your aunt?"

Without giving Emma a chance to answer, Daniel continued in an edgy tone. "Anna Mae was Walter's wife and sister to Emma's father."

Marie hadn't spent the last sixteen years learning how to read people not to know her son was feeling the pressure of their current situation. Feeling the bite of his words, she edged closer to the door, wishing to be anywhere but in the confines of Daniel's truck. For months, all she'd thought about was rebuilding a life with her children. She never considered the life her daughter may have had without her. It was one thing to be an English teenager who was accustomed to the world around them, but to be raised Amish, sheltered and protected from people like her was something she had not considered.

Marie hung her head, embarrassed she hadn't put the two together. "Yes, of course," she said, "now I understand."

Emma looked at her tenderly. "No need to apologize, everything about it is confusing. I can't keep it straight myself."

Trying to lighten the mood, she said, "We'd make a good story, that's for sure."

Daniel laughed at his sister's comment. "Your aunt's or Nathan's?" he asked again.

"I think you can take me home," Emma said. "Anna Mae was worried about me this morning, and I don't want to cause her concern."

Following the well-worn buggy blacktop, Marie took time trying to recall the roads in the town she once called home. The green rolling hills of Tuscarawas County looked much like she remembered. The Amish farms that dotted the landscape gave her a sense of peace that surprised her. Maybe coming back here was a good idea after all.

Hearing the click-click of the turning signal at the exact time she read the street address painted on the white mailbox shook her back to reality. 1042 Troyer Lane.

"STOP."

"What's the matter?" Daniel asked as he pulled off to the side of the driveway.

Barely waiting until he stopped, Marie opened the door and crossed in front of the truck. She stood, glued, and stared at the exact place where her life changed. Closing her eyes, she saw Jake and the Amish man lying on the ground in front of her. She heard Elizabeth crying. Opening her eyes she saw a rock like the one she used to keep her husband from swinging the crowbar at the stranger a second time lay at her feet. Seeing the stone brought back the vivid puddle of blood she continued to see in her dreams. It was as real as the black letters on the mailbox. It was the scene that continued to haunt her in the darkest part of the night.

She heard a soft voice calling her name but didn't respond until Emma touched her shoulder. Jumping at her touch, Marie turned and faced them both. Their confused expressions spoke a million words. Daniel took a deep breath.

"If it's any consolation, I had the same reaction to this spot when I first pulled into this driveway," he said. "I didn't understand why until Anna Mae explained it to me. There are a lot of secrets in this place, but if any of us are going to get past them, we have to leave them, right here in the dirt and gravel."

He didn't know if it was the look of regret in his mother's eyes or the warm way Emma reached out to her, but he felt a connection to the both of them like never before. Maybe his father was right; perhaps it was his job to take care of them.

After dropping Emma off, Daniel didn't go straight to Nathan's. "We're not going to the Bouterights?" Marie asked as they passed the driveway.

"No, I think we need to go shopping first."

"I guess I do look pitiful."

"Not pitiful. Just looks like you could use an outfit that fits you better than the one you have on."

"I suppose so," was all she said as she sat in silence, staring out the window. Memories were clouding her vision at every turn. The Sugar Valley Restaurant where she worked for so many years, the Walnut Creek Mennonite Church her mother took her to as a child, and without Daniel realizing it, the apartment where he'd spent the first five years of his life. Reasoning with herself, she thought. *Could she do this? Could she live in the town that stirred so many memories? If she wanted to make up for all the missed years of her children's lives, she would have to.*

Reaching downtown, Daniel pulled up to the curb in front of Maurice Fashions. He took some money from his wallet and handed it to Marie. "I'll be right here waiting for you when you're done."

She took her time opening the door, thanking him again and promising to be quick.

Listening to the sound of his truck pull away, Marie looked at her reflection in the store's glass windows. Once inside, she took her time getting acclimated to the layout. Seeing the clearance section at the back wall, she walked quietly there, avoiding eye contact with anyone. Pulling two pairs of fitted blue jeans from the rack and a plaid blouse that caught her attention, she headed to the fitting room. Looking at herself in the mirror, she noticed how she had aged. The worry lines on her forehead and the silver strands at her temples reminded her she wasn't the same woman who had fallen in love with the sandy-haired Amish boy with a drinking problem. Slipping on the new clothes, she informed the fitting room attendant she would be wearing them out of the store and asked for the tags to be removed. Carrying the rest of her choices to the counter, she traded a pair of jeans for a skirt at the last minute for a reason she didn't quite understand.

After paying for her purchases, she stood on the sidewalk looking for her son. Within seconds he pulled back up to the curb and she climbed in. Handing Daniel his change, he refused it and told her to keep it in case she needed anything and he wasn't around.

"Thank you. I'll pay you back as soon as I get a job. Speaking of which, can we stop at Sugar Valley? I'd like to see if they need any help. The sooner I find work, the sooner I can get my fines paid and on with life. I don't want to intrude on your friend's hospitality any longer than I have to."

In a surprised voice, Daniel said, "You know you don't have to rush into finding a job today. Give yourself a few days and get your bearings. Why don't you wait at least until after your appointment tomorrow?"

"No, I want to start today."

"Okay, if you're sure."

"I am."

Following her instructions to pull around to the side of the restaurant, he watched as she willed herself to open the door and go inside.

"You don't have to do this today."

"I don't want you or your sister thinking you have to take care of me."

As Marie entered the restaurant, the smell of freshly baked bread and roasted meat surrounded her like a warm hug. If it hadn't been for the owner Andy's kindness all those years ago, she would have never been able to keep Daniel fed. Even when Jake drank her paycheck away it was her boss who was gracious enough to advance her pay to keep a roof over their heads. Walking down the hall and toward the office, she stopped when she saw Andy Kauffman talking to an older gentleman.

Both men stopped and looked her way when they heard her footsteps on the wooden floor.

"Marie, is that you?" Andy asked as he walked to greet her. "I heard you were headed back to Sugarcreek."

Marie found it strange the way he had glanced back at the man as he spoke to her.

The long-bearded man reached out to shake Andy's hand and tipped his black hat to Marie as he passed. "You'll handle the situation we discussed?"

"You can count on it, Bishop."

She got the distinct feeling Andy was expecting her by the way he greeted her.

Stammering on his words, it only took him a few minutes to politely tell her he couldn't or wouldn't hire her back.

Chapter 10 – Settling into Bouteright Stables

Not ready to give up so quickly, Marie had Daniel stop at three more restaurants in town before heading back to Nathan's. All answers were the same. They either didn't need help or knew who she was and weren't willing to take a chance on her.

"Maybe coming back to Sugarcreek was a mistake," she said, climbing back in the truck after another rejection.

"It's just the first day. Don't give up so quickly," Daniel said. "Let people get used to seeing you around again. I find it hard to believe that everyone will be so quick to judge and not give you another chance. Let's get you settled first and worry about a job later."

"But you don't understand," Marie said, her voice cracking. "I have fines to pay, and I refuse to ask you or anyone else to help me with them. I got myself in this mess, and I plan to get myself out."

"I understand that, but let's climb one hill at a time. Right now we need to get you settled at Sarah's."

"Are you sure staying with her is the right thing to do? I know enough about the Amish to know a woman like me wouldn't be the ideal roommate."

"But what you don't understand is Sarah was the first person to welcome you in her home, no questions asked about your past or what you had done. That's because that's what they do. They open their home and hearts to a neighbor in need."

Letting the silence fall between them, Daniel hoped accepting Sarah's offer wasn't a mistake. If Nathan didn't warm up to the idea of Marie being around, he didn't know what he would do. He already knew the small-knit community remembered her and weren't so willing to give her another chance. Could she be right? Was coming back to Sugarcreek the wrong thing to do?

He turned onto the road that led to the familiar red-roofed barns that made up Bouteright Stables. "We're here," he announced.

"Wow," was all Marie said as they drove up the winding driveway.

"It's pretty impressive. Nathan trains horses and delivers them to Amish communities all over the Northeast. Matthew, Emma's brother, maybe opening a holding stable for him in Willow Springs. I love it here and more than that I love working with the horses. Who knows, maybe someday I can do the same."

He stopped in front of the small house to the left of the main house. "This is where Sarah lives. She's expecting you."

As she sat looking out over the beautifully manicured lawn and garden, Marie couldn't help but be amazed by its beauty. She'd driven past the Amish farms that littered the surrounding hills of her hometown as a young woman, but seeing one up close was breathtaking. The pristine small white house looked freshly painted and the red roofs of the three-horse stables shone like polished apples.

Daniel pointed to the house at her right. "Nathan and his mother Rosie live in the big house. Sarah's sister Susan was married to Nathan, but she died over a year ago. Sarah's family sent her here from Willow Springs to take care of their kids, Rachel and Amos. I'm sure you'll meet them soon enough."

Opening the truck door and walking toward the small house, Marie tried to will herself up the stairs to knock on the door. Before she got a chance, a barefoot woman in a purple dress rounded the corner of the house with two small children in tow.

"Marie, welcome. We've been expecting you." Sarah's comforting smile instantly calmed her nerves. Walking between them, Daniel handed his mother the bag of new clothes she had purchased and the small canvas bag she had brought with her.

"You are in good hands with Sarah," he said. "I need to go change my clothes and get to work."

"Okay," Marie said, her voice sheepish. She was not entirely sure she was ready for him to leave.

Sarah could sense Marie's uneasiness and tried to avert her attention.

"Let me introduce you to Nathan's children. This is Rachel and Amos. They were helping me in the garden, but we were stopping to get a snack before Amos laid down for a nap. Would you like to join us?"

Without saying a word, she followed them up the stairs and into Sarah's sparsely furnished house. Pulling the screen door shut behind her, Marie noticed the aroma of warm spice tickling her nose.

"Rachel and I made a batch of gingersnaps this morning before it got too warm," Sarah explained. "They've been wanting to try some all morning. I told them we needed to weed the garden first. Would you like some?"

"Sure," Marie answered quickly.

"Our bedroom is the first door on the right down the hall. You can lay your bags down on the bed if you'd like. Your bed is closest to the window."

Walking in the direction Sarah had pointed, Marie took time adjusting to her new surroundings. The living room opposite the kitchen held only two padded rocking chairs and a small table that sat between them. On the wall hung a calendar and near the window a cuckoo clock much like the one her mother had. The polished floors and white walls looked barren but plenty functional. The small kitchen reminded her of the apartment she and Jake shared when they first got married. The round oak table and its four matching chairs looked identical to the one Jake had made for her as a wedding present. It was the one and only thing he had ever given her.

Chasing the memory from her head, she walked into the bedroom. Two twin beds were placed on opposite walls. Placing her bags on the bed, she took a minute to look out the window overlooking the garden. A row of neatly planted sunflowers and corn that was just starting to tassel out stood looking back at her. Every one of her senses was awakened by the calmness and beauty of Sarah's home.

Walking back into the kitchen, Marie watched Sarah fill glasses of milk and set a plate of cookies in the middle of the table.

Looking up, Sarah said, "Come join us. Rachel says they are the best cookies we've made all summer. We've been playing around with the amount of ginger we add. She claims we got it right this time."

Marie pulled out a chair and ran her hand over the edge of the table. "I love your table," she said. "I had one just like it once."

Sarah smiled. "There are a few furniture makers in Sugarcreek. I'm sure they've made hundreds of them over the years. Is that where you got yours from?"

"No, my husband made it for me as a wedding present. His father taught him how to make furniture when he was young."

Noticing the sound of longing in her voice, Sarah tried to change the subject. "I hope you like to keep busy. These two, plus cooking for all of Nathan's stable hands, keep my days pretty full."

Sarah walked to the stove and held up the coffee pot. "Would you rather a cup of coffee?"

"Yes."

Waiting for the glass percolator to bubble, Sarah didn't miss a beat. She wiped up the milk Amos had spilled and took two coffee mugs from the cupboard.

There was something about the woman Marie liked. Her warm personality was refreshing and for some reason, it calmed her even though the girl was half her age.

For the next fifteen minutes, Marie sat in silence as she listened to Sarah talk about coming to Sugarcreek to care for Nathan's children. She explained about Rosie's arthritis and a little about Nathan's horse training business. She was glad the girl liked to talk because at the moment it was all she could do not to feel overwhelmed by all that had happened that day.

Standing to put her cup in the sink, Sarah shooed the children outside to play. "So, how did it go with Emma this morning?"

"It was a little tense. I'm hoping we can spend some time together to get to know one another better. I don't feel like I handled our first meeting well. She didn't want to come back here with us."

"Give her some time. So much has happened over the last couple of weeks. Her father wasn't too happy that she came here with Daniel."

94

Not sure what to say, Sarah let a few minutes pass as she wiped the table and put the dirty glasses in the sink. Pushing all the chairs back under the table snugly, she said, "I need to go check on Rosie and see what the children are up to. I'll be starting supper shortly. I like to have it on the table by five. Would you like to help or would you rather stay here and relax?"

"If you don't mind, I'll help."

Following her outside and across the yard, Marie looked around to see if she could see Daniel. When she didn't spot him, she walked faster to catch up to Sarah and the children who came running to her as soon as she got outside.

Amos pulled on Sarah's sleeve and she bent down so he could whisper something in her ear as they made their way to the porch. Smiling and looking back at Marie, Sarah said, "I'm sure Marie would love to see the new foal later. How about you and Rachel go play on the swings while we start supper?"

Patting the dark-haired toddler's head and pointing in the direction of the old maple, Sarah walked toward the house.

~~

From the window in his office, Nathan watched as Sarah and Daniel's mother talked to his *kinner*. The knot in the pit of his stomach was only cut short by one of the stable hands interrupting him to ask a question. By the time he finished explaining where they could find the post hole digger, Sarah and Marie were missing from the yard.

Nathan mumbled under his breath. "How can the Bishop see this as a good idea? I don't want that woman anywhere around my *kinner*."

He knew it wasn't the Amish way to pass judgment on someone he barely knew, but the Bishop was asking too much of him to take in someone who had spent a better part of her life behind bars. He had no idea what kind of woman she was, let alone what type of influence she'd have on his *kinner* and on Sarah. He was sure the Bishop wouldn't approve of it, which would have given him a perfect chance to say no. Shaking his head, as he thought to himself.

95

"Suzy wouldn't have offered our home to someone without asking me first."

Not sure who he was more upset with, the Bishop or Sarah.

Walking out of his office promptly at five, Nathan followed the stable hands up the back steps of the house and into the kitchen. Stopping long enough to remove his boots, like he had been taught long ago by his *mamm*, he went straight to the sink to wash his hands. Turning to take the towel Sarah handed him, he looked up only to be eye-to-eye with the English woman. Her height matched his almost perfectly, and he was taken back by her hazel eyes. He didn't say a word, but nodded in her direction and took his seat at the head of the pine planked table.

Turning his attention away from the woman, he asked his *kinner* about their day before bowing his head. He took extra time asking *Gott* to soften his heart to the stranger at his table. Opening his eyes and lifting his head to see Marie looking back at him, he tapped his fork on the side of his plate as everyone lifted their heads in unison.

~~

Watching as everyone sat quietly around the table and lowered their heads, Marie didn't follow suit. Instead, she studied the man at the end of the table. She'd seen the look on his face when he entered the room. One of contempt and distrust. The same look she saw on the face of every restaurant owner she stopped at that afternoon. He didn't need to say a word for her to know he was anything but happy about her being seated at his table. Her gut told her to get up and run, but knowing she had nowhere else to go, she stayed grounded in her seat. Glancing at Daniel across the table helped. He gave her a reassuring smile and added a slice of meatloaf to his plate as it passed by.

Unaware of the heaviness in the air, Rachel looked at her *datt*. "Aunt Sarah said we could take Marie to see the new foal after supper."

Raising an eyebrow in Sarah's direction, Nathan said, "She did, did she?"

"And we're going to show her the kittens under the porch too. They all have their eyes open and are letting us hold them."

In a stern but loving voice, he asked, "Did you get all the chores done Sarah had for you today? I see she had you helping in the garden. Did you finish?"

Taking a bite of the mashed potatoes he'd put on her plate, Rachel faced Sarah. "Did we?"

"You did, and I appreciate the help. If it's good with your *datt* you can show Marie the foal. But only after you eat all of your supper."

Marie watched the exchange between Nathan and his sister-in-law. She could tell Sarah respected his position as head of the family, but there was something in her tone and the way he looked at her that told her there might be more to their story.

Pushing around the food on her plate, she listened as everyone comfortably chatted about their day. The stable hands and Daniel joked about the blisters he got on his hands from working without gloves. And Sarah filled Nathan in on his mother, who decided to take her evening meal in her room.

Being an only child, Marie felt she missed out on big family dinners. Thinking back, Jake came from a large family and had always wanted them to have seven or eight children. At the time, she thought it was a good idea. Once his drinking got out of control the thoughts of having more children was the furthest from her mind.

With thoughts of Jake, her appetite left. Placing her fork down and folding her hands on her lap she wondered if this was how Jake's childhood was. She didn't know much about his family other than he was raised Amish somewhere in Sugarcreek. He had already been baptized when they met. When news of his drinking and involvement with her made it back to his father, his community banned him. Unless he repented and asked for forgiveness, he was forbidden to have any contact with his family. It did nothing but make him drink more. Two months before they married, he changed his last name and swore he'd never have another thing to do with his father or his community again. She couldn't help but think he wouldn't be happy she'd found refuge with the Amish.

Listening to the single bell that chimed it was half past the hour, the sound took her back to her mother's kitchen. Looking up at the clock that hung over the sink, she clearly saw her mother's short stature washing dishes. In her mind, the black veil her mother wore reminded her of her Mennonite upbringing. Going against the wishes of her mother, she accepted the advances of the first boy who paid any attention to her, Jake. His wild ways were known all over town, and even made it back to the church her mother attended.

Blocking out everyone around her, Marie daydreamed about her mother. When Amos pulled on her sleeve, she jumped. Pulling her arm away more forcefully than necessary, he backed away, looking as if she'd scared him.

Turning in her chair to look him in the eyes, she smiled and apologized. "I'm sorry I scared you. You startled me. Are you ready to go see that foal now?"

Amos reached out his hand for hers, to guide her to the barn. Marie hesitated for a moment before putting her hand inside of his. His tiny fingers closed around her hand as the warmth of his soft skin ran shivers up her arm. His short stubby fingers pulled at her heartstrings. She remembered prying Daniel's small hand from hers the day the policewoman pulled him away from her.

Chapter 11 - The Bishop's Visit

Emma quietly crawled out of bed and left a note on the kitchen table, telling Anna Mae where she was going. Anxious to speak to Daniel, she left early hoping to catch him before he started work.

Choosing to stay back to help her aunt preserve pickles, she let Daniel take Marie to her parole appointment by himself. The thought of another four-hour car ride was more than she could stomach.

For a Wednesday morning, walking along the road that led to Sarah's was busier than she had anticipated. More than once she needed to step off to let a car pass. Sugarcreek certainly was busier than the backroads of Willow Springs. It was just past seven and the August sun was already warming her face as it rose over the hill. A car passed and she welcomed the breeze as it made the Queen Anne's Lace dance in the wind. If she were home, she'd pick a bouquet and take them back to her *mamm*. It wasn't summer unless they had vases filled on the kitchen windowsill with stems soaked in red food coloring. They loved to watch how the white flower heads changed to pink as they drank the colored water. Just the thought of it made her miss *Mamm* and her *schwesters*. Clutching the small pink blanket she'd pulled from her suitcase, she hoped to ask Marie about it. For some reason, she wanted to know who embroidered her initials on it.

Turning into the long driveway that led back to the house and stables, she was surprised to see Daniel and one of the farmhands working on replacing a section of fence near the road.

"Emma, what has you out and about so early? Why didn't you call me? I would have come and picked you up so you didn't have to walk."

"Daniel, you know I'm not going to use that phone unless it's an emergency. And I don't consider a two-mile walk a reason to call for a ride."

Daniel turned to the man helping him. "Give me just a minute," he said, and guided Emma away from where they were working. "What are your plans for today?"

"First, I wanted to see how it went yesterday?"

"Okay, I guess. I'll have to drive her to Mayfield once a month for at least a year, and she's not allowed to move from Sugarcreek without getting approval first. We had to give them this address, and they said someone may make a surprise visit at some point. But that's not the half of it. When she asked about her fines, they pulled up her account, and they'd been paid."

"I don't understand. What do you mean they've been paid?"

"Just that, someone already paid them."

"And she has no idea who?"

"No."

"She didn't say much on the way home, and when we got back, I went to work, and she started supper with Sarah. I tried to talk to her last night, but Sarah said she'd already gone to bed, so I let her be."

Emma looked toward the house. "I thought I'd spend some time with her. I promised Anna Mae I'd help with a quilt this afternoon, but I have a few hours this morning. I'm not sure what we'll talk about, but I brought this blanket hoping it will give us something to discuss. I prayed all the way here that God would help me reach out to her. To be quite honest, all I really want to do is go home. But, for some reason, I feel like He is telling me I need to stay. I don't know how I know, but every time I think about going home I see her face and know I need to be here."

Daniel took his gloves out of his back pocket and put them on.

"How can you be so calm about all of this? Your life has just been turned upside down, and you still want to help her?"

"I'm not calm. My insides are all over the place. I want answers. I want to know why *Datt* felt he had to keep me from her and about our biological father. Most of all, I want to know my family and friends will accept me when I go home."

"I know one thing," Daniel said. "You don't need to worry about your family at home; anyone can see how much they care about you."

Picking up the shovel he laid against the fence he said, "I'd better get back to work. I saw her out in the garden, so I know she's up. Good luck."

"Thanks, I might need it."

Walking up to the house, Emma moved to the side of the driveway when she heard the familiar clip-clop behind her. Surprised to see Bishop Shetler pull up beside her, she stopped and walked toward him.

"Emma, what are you doing out and about so early?" he asked.

"I came to talk to Daniel and check on Marie — I mean my mother. How about you?"

"I have some matters to discuss with Nathan. Can I give you a ride up to the house?"

"No, but thank you."

"Remember, my door is always open should you need counsel."

Waving her off with one hand and flipping the reins with the other, Bishop Shetler clicked his tongue to get his horse to move forward.

As he drove away, he thought to himself again. *"It's the eyes."*

~~

Marie was up before sunrise after going to bed so early. The lack of lights in the house, plus the trip back to Mayfield had forced her to retreat to bed shortly after supper. The uncomfortable silence at the supper table made her feel her presence was causing Nathan stress. Sarah tried to assure her it was nothing, but there was a heaviness in the air she couldn't explain. Today she vowed to stay out of everyone's way the best she could. Sarah had already gone to the house to fix breakfast as she headed to the garden. As a child, she and her mother would work in the garden shortly after sunup. It was her favorite part of the day.

The warm soil felt good in her hands, and the weeds were much easier to pull before the sun had a chance to dry out the dirt. Standing to carry the small pile of weeds to the wagon at the edge of the garden, she saw Emma talking to the same man she'd seen at Sugar Valley Restaurant. Not wanting him to see her, she moved to the corner of the house and watched as he tethered his horse to the post in front of Nathan's and went inside. Walking around the side of the house to Sarah's front porch, she watched Emma head her way. Little did her daughter know how much she favored her father. So much so she was sure Emma was the reason why so many vivid memories of Jake were playing in her head. As Emma walked up on the porch to join her, she noticed a pink blanket draped over her arm.

"What do you have there?" Marie asked.

Emma handed the blanket to her.

Marie held it up and then sank in the rocker behind her. "Oh my, I'd forgotten all about this blanket," she said. "My mother's neighbor made this for you when you were born. She knitted it and then embroidered your initials in the corner. Elizabeth Marie Cooper."

Holding the soft blanket up to her face, she closed her eyes and tried to imagine it still had the sweet baby smell it once held. "Where did you find this?"

Emma sat in the chair next to her. Crossing her legs, she rocked the chair in motion and said, "A couple weeks ago, when I turned sixteen."

"Wait. A couple weeks ago? Your birthday was over six weeks ago."

"*Ya*, I just learned that as well. We've celebrated my birthday on July 17th for the last sixteen years. I didn't know any different. There were a lot of things I didn't know about until two weeks ago. Anyways, on my birthday *Datt* gave me a small wooden box that had all of your unopened letters, that blanket, my birth certificate and a picture of Daniel and me in it."

"So, you never read any of my letters?"

"No, I read them all last week."

Handing Emma the blanket back, Marie crossed her arms in front of her and shook her head, trying to make sense of it all.

"You said your birth certificate was in there?"

"It was, why?"

"I don't know how that's possible. I hadn't even received your official birth certificate back from the state yet. It would have gone to my old address. I never gave it another thought until now. You said there was a picture of Daniel too. Can you describe it to me?"

Reaching in her pocket, she pulled out the tattered photo and handed it to her.

Studying the picture, Marie rubbed her thumb over it and handed it back to Emma. "This picture was taken a few days after I brought you home. It was one of the last good days I remember your father having. He was so happy you were a girl. He made Matthew sit on the sofa and hold you so he could take that picture. He carried it in his wallet and showed it to everyone for weeks after you were born. How it ended up in that box is beyond me."

Laying the photo on top of the blanket folded neatly on her lap, Emma lightly tapped her fingertips on the arm of the chair, trying to get enough courage to ask Marie more questions.

"What do you mean it was one of the last good days he had? Was he sick?"

"He was sick but not the kind that could be cured with medicine. Your father was an alcoholic."

Not wanting to paint the real picture of what their life had become, she stopped before letting Emma hear the ugly truth of his abusive behavior.

Just as she was about to ask her mother another question, the screen door slammed across the yard, and she saw Amos head their way. Rachel was close behind carrying a yellow kitten like a baby, trying to keep it secured tightly in her arms.

Leaving the chair to go rescue the kitten, Marie walked toward Rachel to show her how to hold it properly.

"Rachel, cats don't like to lie on their backs. If you want to hold her so she doesn't scratch you, hold her like this."

Emma smiled as she watched Marie tenderly but firmly show the little girl the proper etiquette to holding a cat. The way Emma saw it, Rachel and Amos were just what Marie needed. A simple but uncomplicated life that revolved around holding cats and weeding gardens.

Watching as the cat escaped Rachel's grip, they both took off chasing it around the side of the house and toward the barn.

~~

Sarah poured the Bishop a fresh cup of coffee and cut him a slice of the cinnamon coffee cake she'd made for breakfast as they waited for Nathan. She had sent Amos to fetch him. She hoped he hadn't got sidetracked on the way.

"What brings you out so early this morning?" Sarah asked as she continued to clear the breakfast dishes from the table.

"I wanted to see how everyone was faring with Daniel's mother here," he replied.

"I enjoy having her here. It's only been a couple days, and she hasn't settled in yet, but I bet it won't take her long," Sarah said. "Amos seems smitten with her, and maybe that's what she needs. Someone other than an adult to connect with."

Scratching his chin, the Bishop sipped his coffee. "Might be right," he said, "*kinner* often can reach people most adults can't."

After a pause, the Bishop continued, "I met Emma along the driveway. It's good to see her visiting with Marie."

Sarah moved to look out the window. "Emma's here? I didn't know that."

She saw Nathan come up the stairs and heard him stomp the barn dust off the bottom of his boots. "Here's Nathan now. I'll leave the two of you to talk and go sit with Rosie for a spell."

As Nathan entered the kitchen, he watched the Bishop push himself away from the table and start to stand.

"Don't get up, stay put. What do I owe this visit to?" Nathan asked as he pulled his chair out and sat across from him.

"I was in the area and wanted to stop in and see how things were going with your new house guest."

"In the area? You live two miles down the road, you're always in the area."

"Okay, so I wanted to see how things were going. Is Daniel's mother settling in?"

In an aggravated voice, Nathan answered. "I haven't said two words to her, so if you want to know how she's doing, you'll need to ask Sarah."

Nathan drummed his fingers on the table. His frustration was building by the Bishop's desire to talk about Marie. "Like I said on Sunday, I'm not too happy she's here, but if you feel I need to do my neighborly duty by providing her a place to stay, I'll do as you wish."

Taking the last bite of cake from his plate and pushing it away, the Bishop looked sternly at Nathan. "I not only want you to provide her room, but I also want you to give her a job."

"You want me to do what?"

"You heard me. I want you to give her a job."

Trying not to lose his temper or raise his voice to the man who had held him up since his *fraa* died, he repeated the man's words again. "You want me to give her a job?"

"I do. The Ministers and I feel it's time Sarah go back to Willow Springs. We want you to hire Marie to care for your *kinner* and *mamm*."

"You can't be serious?"

"I can, and I am."

With that, Bishop Shetler pushed himself away from the table and retrieved his hat from the back of the chair. Stopping only for a second before he walked to the door, he said, "I expect you'll see to it promptly."

Nathan didn't move from his chair. Lost in his own thoughts, he didn't hear Sarah come back into the room and to the table.

"Are you all right?" she asked in a concerned tone. "I can't say I ever remember Bishop Shetler visiting so early in the day. I hope all is well."

He stood to look her in the eye. "No, all isn't well. He came to tell me it was time for you to go home."

"Go home? What are you talking about? What about the *kinner*, who will take care of them? And your *mamm*, who is going to help her?"

"I'm to hire Marie to take over."

Without so much as an explanation, he left, slamming the screen door so hard it rattled the windows.

Sarah sank in her chair at the table and tried to make sense of it all. Why would the Bishop want Marie to take her place? How was she ever going to leave the *kinner*? A big part of her was happy she could go home to Matthew and couldn't help but think this was the answer to her prayers. Was *Gott* guiding her footsteps back to Willow Springs? Even though she was heartsick about telling the *kinner*, she had to believe Marie coming here was all part of *Gott's* plan. Why else would the Bishop send her away at this very moment?

~~

In less than two days, Nathan had arranged for a driver to take Sarah home and offered Marie a job as his housekeeper and nanny. Because he was unsure of her capabilities, he asked Emma to help out for a few weeks until Marie got the hang of working without all the modern conveniences of an English home. Rachel and Amos took it the worse. It was like all three of them were thrown back into a state of grieving. For over a year Sarah had been there to pick up the pieces of their broken hearts.

Saying goodbye to Sarah was harder than he imagined it would be. If he was honest with himself, he knew it was best. Maybe the Bishop did him a favor because he was sure Sarah's resemblance to his late *fraa* was more of a comfort to him than anything else. He wasn't blind to see Sarah didn't hold the same affection for him as he did for her. But again, was it love or just a yearning for anything that resembled Suzy? In the end, he knew Bishop Shetler must have seen right through him. Why else would he have insisted she go back to her family in Willow Springs? It didn't matter now. Sarah was gone, and he was left to trust Marie Cooper with his *kinner* and the care of his home. He couldn't tell a soul, but he secretly prayed, she'd fail terribly, and he could let her go as fast as he hired her.

~~

To be closer to Marie and to help as much as she could, Emma moved into the *doddi haus* at Nathan's. She had concluded her best shot at helping her mother find her place in the world would be working side by side with her. She played over and over in her head the words Daniel said. *"Take it one hill at a time."* She intended to do just that. Her first hill was to teach her mother how to cook on a wood-fired stove. Nathan's Church District was a bit more liberal than hers in Pennsylvania, but they still cooked with wood.

Standing on the porch and watching Rachel ride her bike she smiled as she remembered Daniels promised to help her learn to ride. In Willow Springs bicycles were forbidden. But in Sugarcreek her feet were itching to discover the mystery of balancing herself on two wheels. Maybe it was the *rumshpringa* coming out in her, but she was determined to ride before she went home.

Chapter 12 - Breakfast

Staring up at the ceiling, Marie tried to clear her mind enough to fall asleep. Sarah had left the night before, and Emma fell asleep long ago in the bed across the room. As she watched the moon bounce shadows off the wall, she worried she wouldn't be able to catch on quick enough to suit Nathan. Thank goodness Emma agreed to help. It was one thing to take care of two small children, but it was another thing to run a home and cook without electricity and modern appliances. Nathan hadn't told her, but she was good enough at reading people to know he wasn't thrilled with the new arrangement. She hesitated about accepting his offer but felt she had no other choice.

Six o'clock would come too soon if she didn't close her eyes. Try as she may, she couldn't sleep. Quietly leaving the darkened room, she grabbed the quilt off the bed and headed to the porch. Wrapping herself in the hand-stitched purple and white bundle, she pulled her knees up to her chest and sat in the rocker closest to the door. Listening to a distant owl and the soft neighing of a horse in the stables, she waited for her eyes to get accustomed to the dark. A movement to her left caught her eye as she watched Nathan walk to the edge of the porch across the yard. The moon was full and bright, and she could make out his slender outline. Too dark to see if he could see her, she stayed still, not wanting to bring attention to herself. It was late, and it could only mean neither of them had peace about what tomorrow might bring. From the darkness of her hidden corner she watched as he dropped to sit on the top step of the wraparound porch. Not sure what to make of him, she pulled the quilt tighter and nodded off.

~~

Standing at the screened door, Nathan welcomed the breeze that swirled in the room through the mesh. One hand wrapped firmly around a coffee mug, he stood looking out into the night. The *kinner* had long gone to bed, his *mamm* was fast asleep, and the only sounds to be heard were those of the nighttime creatures that surrounded the farm. Softly opening the door to retreat to the porch, he stood in the darkness missing Sarah. Or, was he missing Suzy? The two intertwined in his mind so tightly he could never be sure which. As a respected member of his Amish Community he had no choice but to follow the demands put on him by the Bishop and the Ministers. If he felt they didn't have just cause in sending Sarah home he would have spoken up. But down deep, he knew it was time, no matter how upset Rachel and Amos had been. Maybe the Bishop knew him better than he knew himself. Besides sending her away he was more concerned with what he was going to do about Marie Cooper. They had yet to exchange more than a dozen words and the thoughts of her spending so much time with his *kinner* made him uncomfortable. Thank goodness Emma would be around. That at least gave him a little peace. But then again, he didn't know anything about Daniel's sister either. Taking the last sip of his now cold coffee, he pushed his hair off his forehead and thought. *"How did I end up with the whole mess of 'em? Some family — none of them even have the same last name."*

Shaking his head, he stood and headed back inside, stopping long enough to look up at the moon and say a little prayer. *"Gott, I'm not sure what you have planned here, but you're going to have to help me with this one."*

~~

Emma heard the buzz of the alarm and wondered why her mother wasn't shutting it off. Rolling out of bed and walking to the clock, she was surprised to see Marie gone. Walking to the kitchen, she was confused when she was nowhere in sight. Turning the wick up on the oil lamp hung above the table she struck a match to bring light to the room. The soft glow threw light on the porch enough that she noticed the edge of the quilt from her mother's bed lying on the floor. Opening the door and putting her hand on her mother's shoulder, she shook her lightly. Marie bolted from the chair so fast she got her legs tangled in the blanket and fell to the floor. Emma reached out to help her up, but she refused to take her hand.

"I'm sorry I startled you. Here let me help you."

"No, I'm fine," Marie said, quickly gathering herself up. "I don't need your help."

Feeling the blow of her mother's words, Emma turned and went back inside.

Trying to make sense of what happened, Emma quickly dressed, trying to stay out of her mother's way. *Maybe she wasn't a morning person like Rebecca*, she thought to herself. Thinking of how her *schwester* sometimes acted gave her a little justification in her mother's behavior.

Lighting the lamp on the stand near the bed, Emma sat with her back to the door, brushing the tangles out of her hair enough so it could be twisted in a bun at the nape of her neck. Taking a straight pin and working it through the hairpin on top of her head, she secured the stiff *kapp* in place.

"I used to watch my mother pin her hair up in almost the same way."

Turning toward Marie's voice, Emma half expected an apology, but one never came. Wondering if she should comment on the scene from the porch, she hesitated and decided to forget it happened. Curious about her grandmother, she asked, "She wore her hair in a bun?"

"Yes," Marie answered, grabbing the pair of jeans that lay over the foot of her bed.

Before Emma could even think of another question, Marie was gone.

Oh my, it's going to be a long day, Emma thought, rubbing her forehead with her fingers. *What did I get myself into?*

~~

Emma let Marie do more watching than anything else when it came to making breakfast for such a large group. Cooking for ten people three times a day was quite a chore. The four stable hands worked up quite an appetite, including Daniel, and she wasn't sure how Sarah did it by herself. For sure and certain they both were going to have their hands full. As she stood at the stove making scrambled eggs, Marie fumbled her way around the kitchen looking for what she needed to set the table. Showing her how to light the stove and fill the oil lamps would have to wait until breakfast was finished.

After Marie had got everything down from the cupboards, Emma pointed to the steps. "I'm sure Sarah got the children up and downstairs for breakfast by the time Nathan came back up from the barn. Maybe you should get them up. We should check on Rosie too. She might need help getting dressed."

Marie stood at the bottom of the steps, half afraid to go upstairs. Could she do this? She couldn't even take care of her own children; how was she ever going to take care of someone else's?

At the last minute, she decided to go through the living room and check on Rosie first. She had been briefly introduced to the old woman the night before and wasn't too sure how she felt about her. Knocking on the door before she pushed it open, she peeked inside to see the woman trying to run a brush through her long hair. Rosie's hands were pulled in crippled fists, and she was trying to get a good grip on the handle.

The front of her dress lay open, exposing her undergarment as she tried to pull it close with one hand. Frustration etched on her brow, a single tear fell down her cheek as the brush she held fell to the floor.

"I feel so useless, my hands have a mind of their own," Rosie said in her gravelly voice. "With Sarah gone I need to go help the *kinner*."

Picking the brush up off the floor, Marie stood in front of the woman trying to figure out what to do first. The pile of pins on the nightstand was waiting to be used to close her dress as was the *kapp* on her bed.

"I'll be right back," Marie said, turning to get Emma.

111

Hoping Emma could trade places with her she headed to the kitchen only to find Nathan and the men taking their seats.

Meeting the glare of Nathan as soon as she walked in the room, he said. "Why aren't Rachel and Amos up yet?"

"I was headed to get them, but Rosie needed help first."

Walking past him and straight to Emma, she leaned in and whispered in her ear. "Rosie needs help getting dressed."

Not lifting her head from the pot of oatmeal, Emma said in a hushed tone. "Then help her."

"But the pins and her head covering. I don't know what to do."

Emma tried not to seem frustrated by her mother's inability to help Rosie. "Okay," she instructed, "finish the oatmeal."

Nathan picked his cup off the table and walked near the stove. "Are you going to get Rachel and Amos up, or am I going to have to do it?"

"Yes, of course, I'll go right now."

Putting the spoon on the stove and pushing the pot to the back burner, Marie headed to the stairs. At the top, she saw both children had come from their rooms, rubbing the sleep from their eyes.

"Rachel, Amos, thank goodness you're awake. Your father wants you both downstairs for breakfast."

Ushering the children to their seats, Marie smelled something burning. Rushing to the stove, she grabbed the pot off the back burner. But with no potholder, she instantly dropped it, splashing hot oatmeal all over the floor. The pain in her hand sent her to the sink while Daniel wasted no time cleaning up the mess.

Running her hand under cold water, she took a deep breath, not wanting to turn around and face the eyes she felt burning her back. Feeling a tug on her shirttail, she glanced down to see Amos holding up a small green can of salve. Taking the square can from his hand, Marie watched him return to his seat without a word. Applying the balm and wrapping her hand in a towel, she continued to put breakfast on the table.

Emma had walked Rosie to the kitchen, all dressed and ready for the day. The air in the room was as thick as the Bag Balm Marie used to soothe her burn. No one said a word as Nathan bowed his head. Dutifully, Emma and Daniel had both dropped their heads.

112

The only person other than Marie who still had their head high was Amos. He was looking her way, and as quickly as she caught his eye he smiled and lowered his head. Closing her eyes and following suit she prayed, something she hadn't done in a very long time. "God, what am I doing here? I don't belong with these people." It was not so much a prayer but a plea for understanding. As if on cue everyone picked up their heads the minute Nathan rattled his silverware. Being the last one to look up she caught Nathan looking her way.

"How is your hand?" he asked, adding apple butter to a slice of toast.

Because he hadn't said more than two words to her since she arrived, other than to ask her about filling Sarah's shoes, Marie was taken aback by his concern. "It'll be fine. I'm sorry I burned the oatmeal."

"None of us will go hungry" was all he said as he went back to eating.

Listening to the morning conversation between the stable hands and Nathan broke up the tension in the room. Emma helped Rosie, and she took care of filling the children's plates.

Nathan took the last sip of his coffee and looked toward the coffee pot on the stove. Being a waitress for so many years, Marie was in tune with his needs. Without even asking she took his cup and filled it. Sitting it on the corner of the table, she stirred in two teaspoons of sugar and a splash of milk just like she had seen him do earlier. Handing it back to him she averted her eyes and went back to helping Amos cut his sausage.

Out of the corner of his eye, Nathan watched Marie. He felt responsible for her burn. If he hadn't been so adamant she get the children up she wouldn't have left the pot on the stove. He couldn't help but watch her nervous behavior. A little part of him softened when Amos went to her so quickly. It was going to take him some time to warm up to the idea of having her in his home, but maybe *Gott* was trying to show him how to look at her through the eyes of a child. His son surely didn't care that she was English. Through his eyes she was just Marie. Pushing his plate away he leaned back in his chair and picked up his cup. Savoring the hot liquid, he thought, *she's at least observant. She made my coffee just as I like it.*

113

It hadn't been but thirty minutes when the stable hands and Nathan left to start their day. Emma and Rosie hadn't moved from their places at the table, and Rachel and Amos were still finishing the food in front of them. Marie hadn't touched her food but stood to pour herself another cup of coffee. Standing at the sink she watched the men walked across the yard and disappeared to the stables. It had been years since she'd been around men. They made her nervous, especially Nathan. There was something about him that reminded her of Jake. The Jake she knew before a bottle consumed his life and before he was banned from his family. A quiet, confident man — much like Nathan. Shaking her head to push the memories away, she turned to Emma. "So, what's on our agenda today?"

Emma looked at Rosie. "I think if you can tell us how Nathan likes things and what Sarah did each day, we will know where to start. For sure and certain we don't want another morning like the one we had today."

Marie listened intently as Rosie explained how Nathan wanted the children dressed and ready for breakfast promptly at seven. How he liked his dinner at twelve-thirty and supper at five. She described how he took the children to the Horse and Tack Auction every Friday and how Sarah went with him. She went into great detail on how he liked to take his coffee to the porch every evening and how he tucked Rachel and Amos in at night.

"My boy has a rough exterior, but don't let that scare you," she said tenderly. "He loves his family and treats those stable boys like his own."

Rosie reached for her cup with both hands, carefully bringing it to her mouth. "I'm not much help around here anymore. But my mind is good, and I'll help as much as I can."

Marie knew enough about people to see if she were going to make this situation work she would need to rely on Rosie's help. She had no other choice. Emma could teach her how to run an Amish home, but Rosie could teach her how to earn Nathan's trust.

Rosie put her hands on her lap and looked at Marie. "One more thing," the small woman said, "he will expect you to go to Church."

Not sure what to say, Marie looked to Emma for any sign of guidance.

"I don't think you'll have a choice," Emma said as she started to clear the table. "If you're living under his roof and one of his employees, it's what he expects of you. How can you go against that?"

"But an Amish church service?" Marie was aghast. "The community will never welcome me."

Rosie wasted no time in commenting. "It's not up to any of us to judge you. If you are a member of Nathan's household, it's what is required."

Marie didn't know how to respond. It had been too many years since she went to church. She didn't even go to the Sunday services at Mayfield. The hurt was always too raw. God had abandoned her a long time ago, and she didn't feel she owed Him anything, especially sitting through the three-hour church services Jake had told her about.

Looking across the table, she felt a sense of peace listening to the older woman talk. The way she carried herself and the sweet tone she used reminded her of her own mother.

"Child, we must not be afraid to place an unknown future in the hands of God," Rosie said. "There is a purpose for you here. It is not our job to question His plan, only to be obedient to it."

Laying her hand on Emma's arm, Rosie pointed to her chair in the other room, indicating she was finished at the table.

Marie watched as Emma helped Rosie into the sitting room and thought. *Was this all part of God's plan? Why would God have any interest in my life?*

Chapter 13 - A Child's Touch

Emma stood in the arched doorway that separated the kitchen from the sitting room, wondering what she should show her mother first. There was so much for her to learn if she was going to run Nathan's household. It was Thursday, laundry was piling up, the *kinner* needed dressed, the kitchen was a mess, and they used the last of the bread for breakfast. It would have been nice if the Bishop would have let Sarah stay long enough to explain how Nathan liked things, but she was just going to have to use the same schedule her *mamm* had used.

Scraping the plates into one of the empty bowls on the table, she said, "Rosie said Rachel and Amos have chores. Rachel gathers eggs, and Amos feeds the barn cats."

"We have to make our beds and brush our teeth too," Rachel was quick to add, before taking the last sip of her milk.

Emma took the towel from the counter to wipe the jelly from Amos's cheek and told them to go get dressed. Carrying a stack of plates to the sink, she continued to explain all they needed to get accomplished before starting dinner.

Marie hadn't said a word or moved from her chair since her daughter left to get Rosie settled. Turning from the sink to look at her mother and wait for a response, the blank stare on her face spoke louder than any words could describe.

Pulling out the chair beside her, Emma sat, trying to find words to ease her anxiety. "I'm sure Nathan realizes it's going to take more than one meal for things to get into a rhythm around here."

Marie wrapped the wet dishcloth around her hand tighter. "That's not what worries me," she said, looking down. "I can tell he's not comfortable with me being here. I'm confident I can cook his meals and clean his house, but if he's not going to trust me with his children and his mother, that's another issue altogether. I can't say I blame him. How would any father want his children around me?"

Emma reached out for her mother's hand to see the burn. Marie pulled her hand back and placed it in her lap.

Emma let it go as the scene on the porch entered her mind. Immediately connecting the two, she thought, *That's it. She doesn't like to be touched.* Sitting back in her chair, she waited for her mother to continue to tell her what was on her mind.

Marie shifted in her chair. "Maybe this was a bad idea. I've put both you and Daniel in a difficult situation. You should be back in Willow Springs with your family, and your brother left his job to come help me. I should have never asked him to find you. You were much better off without me."

Not sure what to say, Emma said a silent prayer asking *Gott* to help her find the words her mother needed to hear. She didn't know what she expected, but she didn't think her mother would be in such a fragile state. Her *mamm* was so strong and sure of herself, she never had to worry about picking her up. With Marie it had become apparent that she would need to be the strong one and carry her. How she was going to do that she wasn't sure, but one thing for certain was she'd need to rely on *Gott's* help. To start with she needed to set her straight.

"If Daniel and I didn't want to be here, we wouldn't be. We decided together to help you, so that is just crazy talk."

Stopping long enough to gather her thoughts before getting back to clearing the table, Emma continued, "I don't know anything about your life other than what you shared with me in your letters. But I know enough that you've taken the blame for so many things that maybe you had no control over. The way I look at it, Nathan has no cause not to trust you. He doesn't know the whole story. Maybe you should explain it to him."

Marie stood to carry the empty coffee mugs to the sink. "I can see it in his face when he looks at me. I don't think explaining it to him will do any good. To him, I'm just an English woman he's been forced to take in. All Amish are the same."

117

Bothered by her comment, Emma turned toward her mother. "What do you mean all the same?"

"It's the same look Jake's mother gave me when she found out I was pregnant. Your father took me to see her once. He was so excited he couldn't help but find a way to see her, even after his father had banned him from his family. I'll never forget the way she looked at me. It's the same way Nathan looked at me this morning. Like I'll never be good enough. Not even good enough to clean his house and cook his meals."

Emma chose her words carefully before commenting on her mother's observation.

"The way I see it, you're doing the same thing. You're judging Nathan before you've given him a chance. You're comparing him to the way one Amish woman treated you. If my father took you to see his mother while he was in the *ban,* her reaction probably had more to do with him putting her in a sensitive situation than anything else."

Running water in the sink and waiting for it to fill up, Emma tried to figure out how she was going to deal with her mother's negative attitude. It was all too much to try and figure out in a few days. All she knew was they had a job to do, and they needed to get busy. Maybe Daniel would have some ideas. Together they could help her build enough confidence in herself to adjust to her new life — on an Amish farm.

The sound of tiny feet echoing on the stairs brought their attention back to the children. Amos stopped in front of Marie, and without so much of a word, he turned her hand over, kissed her palm and was out the door.

Emma watched as the discouraged look on her mother's face softened. She wasn't sure she would be able to break through the wall her mother had built, but it looked like Amos might be the one to slip inside her heart.

Marie spent the morning watching and listening to Emma explain how to use the gas generator that ran the washing machine, how to add kindling to the cookstove, how to use straight pins to fasten Rosie's dress together and she even showed her how to add

118

oil to the lamp above the table. The morning flew by, and before they knew it, they were back in the kitchen preparing dinner.

"Oh no," Emma said as she saw the empty wicker breadbasket. "We needed to make bread this morning. We don't have enough for dinner."

Marie opened the cupboard, pulled out a small red can of baking soda, and grabbed a bowl off the shelf. "No problem, we can make biscuits. They won't take no time at all."

Emma watched as her mother took the lead in helping with dinner. Marie had spent all morning following her around, and it was great to see her throw herself into something … even if it was making biscuits.

Rachel and Amos were sitting quietly at the table coloring as they started dinner. As soon as Marie flipped the sticky dough on the counter, Rachel left her crayons and dug through the drawer beside her. When she found the round tin biscuit cutter, she pushed her chair over to Marie.

"*Mamm* said this was my job," Rachel said, a longing in her voice. Marie sprinkled flour on the dough, rolled it out to the perfect thickness and motioned to Rachel to start cutting them out.

"How about the next time we make biscuits you do it all?"

"Really? I can make them myself?"

"I'd say if your mother trusted you to cut them out, it's time you learned how to make them from start to finish."

For the next hour, Emma watched as Rachel followed Marie around the kitchen. For someone who hadn't worked in her own kitchen for sixteen years, Marie was no stranger to putting a meal on the table. The room was beginning to fill with the wonderful smells of brown sugar meatloaf and butter-topped biscuits. Quite a change from the disaster breakfast had been. With all the commotion in the kitchen, Rosie called for Emma to help her to the rocking chair in the corner. When the table was set and the creamy potatoes placed in a bowl, all that was left to do was drizzle honey on top of the warm biscuits.

Holding the honey jar up for Rachel to see, Marie waved her over to finish the job. Showing her only once how to use the wooden honey dipper to lightly drizzle the golden sweetness over the warm biscuits, she left to fill a pitcher with cold water. No sooner had Rachel stepped down from the chair when Nathan and his crew came in the back door. Each of them took their manure-caked boots off, leaving them in a row just outside the door.

"Something smells wonderful," Daniel said, walking into the room. Taking off his baseball cap and hanging it on the peg next to the row of straw hats, he took his seat and waited for everyone to follow suit.

Nathan barely got to his seat when Rachel ran up to him to tell him she had cut out the biscuits just like her *Mamm* had taught her.

Marie watched as Nathan took the time to listen to his daughter. She could see his love for her was genuine, and he took an interest in what she had to say. A part of his demeanor reminded her of how Jake had been with Daniel in the very beginning. He loved to hold him and wanted to learn how to be a good father. As time went on and his drinking got worse, the resentment and exclusion from his family turned him to a mean and spiteful man she didn't know. She wondered if Nathan had a mean streak in him. It really didn't matter because she vowed she'd never let any man get that close to her again, especially not another Amish man.

After everyone found their places, Marie watched as every head dropped and wondered what each prayer held. Glancing around the table, she stopped at Nathan who was looking back at her. For what seemed like minutes, they both stared at each other not saying a word. If she was going to gain his trust this wasn't how to do it. He continued to watch her as he picked up his fork and tapped it on the side of his glass.

Nathan took a bite of the meatloaf. "This is good," he said, looking at Emma.

Emma passed the basket of biscuits to Rachel. "That's Marie's recipe, not mine. I didn't know what to think when she dug out the brown sugar and ketchup, but I can see it's a hit."

Not waiting for Emma to finish, Rachel interrupted. "Marie said I can make biscuits all by myself next time."

Taking a biscuit from the wicker basket she held, Nathan raised an eyebrow. "She did, did she? Whose idea was the honey?"

"You don't like the honey, *Datt*?" Rachel had an unsureness in her voice.

"Now I didn't say that. In fact, I think from now on, that's the only way I want them."

With a pleased smile on her face, Rachel went back to eating, happy her *Datt* liked the biscuits.

For the rest of the meal, Marie avoided making eye contact with him. She'd make it a point not to let him catch her not bowing her head again.

Listening to the men chat about what they needed to accomplish that afternoon helped ease the uneasiness she felt about Nathan. Looking for any excuse to leave the room, she was glad to see Amos falling asleep in his potatoes.

Taking a napkin from the Lazy Susan in the middle of the table, she wiped his face and picked him up from his chair. She looked at Emma and nodded her head in the direction of the stairs, telling her she was lying him down for a nap.

Nestling his head on her shoulder, Marie couldn't help but pull him close as she carried him up the stairs. When she got to his room she sat in the rocker near the window and held him until she was sure he was fast asleep. Gently rubbing his back, she hummed a song she used to put Daniel to sleep. Leaning her head back against the rocker, she closed her eyes, trying to push out the memories Amos stirred in her. It had been too many years since she'd felt another person's touch, but for some reason, Amos felt good in her arms. The feeling that she needed to protect him was overwhelming. But, protect him from what, she had no idea. She didn't need to keep him safe from Nathan, that was sure. Maybe he reminded her of all the time she'd lost with her own children and how she needed to keep them safe from Jake. The softness of his hair and the way he felt in her arms just felt right. But it wasn't right, he wasn't her child, and she'd never get back what God took away from her. Another reason why even a prayer at dinner wouldn't work for her.

Waiting until she heard the squeaky screen door slam before going back downstairs, Marie laid Amos on his bed and closed the door softly. Taking a minute to make sure he wasn't going to wake up, she stood in the hallway across from Nathan's room. Without even thinking she walked to the open door and looked inside. The familiar Wedding Star patterned quilt was neatly pulled up over the pillows, and everything was in its place. A navy blue dress hung on the peg beside the window, and a crisp white *kapp* sat on the dresser beside a hairbrush. If she didn't know any better, she'd think a woman still shared his room. Looking back to the bed she walked in and ran her fingers over the quilt. The pattern was much like the quilt she and Jake had received after they married. They never did find out who sent it. She wondered whatever happened to it. The gray double wedding ring design was offset by maroon-colored fabric, much like she remembered hers to be. The only difference was her star was baby blue instead of maroon. She studied the tiny hand-stitched designed on the white background and felt a connection to it she couldn't explain.

Hearing the pat of tiny feet on the hardwood stairs, Marie quickly went out to meet Rachel.

"Marie, there you are. I was looking for you. *Mommi* is asking for you and Emma sent me to find you. Emma was going outside to take clothes off the line and said she'd help you clean the kitchen when she gets back inside."

Putting her finger to her lips, Marie hushed the child and directed her down the stairs. "What does Rosie need?"

"I don't know, Emma just told me to get you."

"Okay, how about we find out together."

Rosie had been moved to the chair near the window and had her lap covered in a small blanket with a tube of ointment on the stand next to her. Looking up as they entered the room, she was quick to point to the cream.

Plugging her nose, Rachel pointed to the cream. "Oh no. That stinks. I'm not going anywhere near it."

"That's okay. How about you go help Emma with the clothes and I'll help Rosie." Marie said as she headed in Rosie's direction.

Still plugging her nose, Rachel backed away. "Good, because that smells bad."

Marie pulled one of the rockers along with the small braided rug beneath it in front of Rosie. She squeezed a small dot from the tube into the palm of her hand. Hesitating, Marie had to force herself to reach out and pick up Rosie's claw-like fingers. It was one thing to hold Amos close, but touching an adult was another thing altogether.

Rosie's skin was soft and silky. Marie tried to push the thoughts of Jake's rough and calloused fingers around her wrists out of her mind. Instead she massaged the cream into Rosie's knuckles, trying to keep her anxiety in check. As quickly as she could get the ointment evenly applied, she reached for a tissue to wiped the excess off her hands.

Before she had a chance to retreat back to the kitchen, Rosie leaned in closer to Marie. In almost a whisper, she said, "Sometimes we want answers, but if we get them all at once there's no need for us to have faith. The only way we know something is in God's plan is to compare it to His word."

Marie didn't know what to say, so she patted the top of the old woman's hand and left the room.

Alone in the kitchen, she played Rosie's words over in her head. *"Faith, I lost that a long time ago. How can leading me back to Sugarcreek to face everything that reminds me of a time I want to forget be in God's plan?*

Moving to the sink to fill it with water, she looked out the window to the landscape in front of her. If nothing else, this place had a calming effect on her like no other place had ever had. For that she would be thankful. As for Rosie's words, they didn't make sense and she wasn't going to waste time trying to figure them out.

Chapter 14 - Pedal Like This

For the next few days, Marie and Emma fell into a familiar routine of preparing meals and taking care of Rachel, Amos, and Rosie. Nathan spent more time than usual away from the farm, which Marie gladly accepted. Whenever he was close, the tension between them was inevitable. He did all he could do to stay away from her, but more than once she caught him watching her from a distance.

Sunday afternoon, instead of visiting another church district on their off Sunday, Nathan told them they would be spending the day at home. The *kinner* were playing in the shade of the big maple tree in the side yard, and Rosie was enjoying a slight summer breeze in the rocking chair on the porch. Nathan had excused Marie and Emma from making dinner and told them he would care for his *kinner* for the rest of the day.

Marie was more than happy to take the day off and even more relieved she didn't have to attend church. She had withstood much that week and didn't think she had it in her to hold her head high while being scrutinized by prying eyes. It was only a matter of time before she'd have to attend, but the reprieve was welcomed for the day.

Sitting on the small porch across the yard, she watched as Nathan pulled up a chair next to his mother. A part of her wondered if they were talking about her, but down deep, she didn't want to know what he thought of her. Why she concerned herself with what he might or might not think frustrated her. She was there to do a job and nothing else.

Pushing her rocking chair in motion, she closed her eyes and breathed in summer. The smell of freshly cut hay lingered in the air as the surrounding farms had taken advantage of the hot days to complete that important chore. The sounds of summer filled her ears—the chirping of crickets, cicadas, and a distant songbird played a symphony for her. For a few minutes, she allowed herself to enjoy the peacefulness that surrounded her. Then, the screened door slammed. Jolted back to reality, Marie opened her eyes to see Emma standing before her, offering a glass of iced tea.

Taking it, she was as polite –and independent—as ever. "Thank you, but you didn't need to wait on me."

Emma sat in the chair beside her. "When are you going to realize little things like bringing you something to drink is what family does for each other?"

Not commenting, Marie sipped the minty drink. She didn't want to offend her daughter again. It was going to take time getting used to letting someone, even her children, do something for her.

Trying to change the subject, she asked, "Where did Daniel go?"

"I'm not sure, he said he had a surprise for me and he'd be back shortly."

The words had barely left her lips when Daniel's truck came up the driveway and pulled up close to the porch. He hollered in Emma's direction: "Are you ready?"

"Ready for what?" Emma asked, rising and walking to the end of the porch.

"For your first lesson."

He pulled a yellow bike from the bed of his truck, put the kickstand down and looked her way.

"Oh my, are you serious?"

"As your big brother, I must teach you how to ride a bike. I wouldn't want to shirk my duties."

Running down the steps, Emma stopped to slide her hand across the shiny silver handlebars. "I'm not sure I can do this, but I certainly want to give it a try."

Daniel looked down at his sister's bare feet. "You might want to put on a pair of shoes. Those foot pedals will be hard on your feet."

"Okay, I'll be right back."

Daniel turned when he heard Rachel come up behind him, asking who got a new bike.

"It's Emma's. Do you like it?"

"It's pretty and it matches my dress," the child said, pointing to the buttercup-colored fabric.

"That it does. Would you like to help me teach her how to ride it?"

"Can I?"

"You can. How about you go get your bike? If Emma sees how easily you can ride yours, she might not be so scared to learn."

Smiling at Rachel's eagerness to help, Daniel watched as she ran across the yard to retrieve her bike from the side of the porch.

Marie moved to the edge of the steps and in a *questioning* tone, asked. "Your father taught you, do you remember?"

"No, I can't say I do."

"You cried something awful when he took off your training wheels. But as soon as he let go of your seat, you took off with no problem. You only fell once. You didn't get the hang of using the brakes right away and ran into the side of my car."

Laughing at his mother's story, Daniel watched as Emma came back outside, sporting her black sneakers.

"I'm ready."

"And here comes your co-pilot," he said, looking toward Rachel riding up to meet them. "Wait, let me move my truck," he added, and winked in his mother's direction. "I'd hate for you to run into it."

Emma stood beside the bike as she listened to Rachel explain all she needed to do.

"First, you need to stand between it, like this. Hold the handles and put your foot on the pedal."

Emma followed the little girl's instructions and copied everything she told her to do.

"And then you just push the pedal and ride."

With that, Rachel pedaled her bike out into the driveway, made a big circle, and stopped beside Emma.

Daniel walked up beside them. "See? As simple as that. You got it?"

Emma was honest. "I'm not so sure I can do all of that so quickly. But Rachel makes it look simple."

"It's easy, Emma, just try," Rachel said as she took off again. "Pedal like this."

They all watched as Rachel made her way around the circular driveway past Nathan's house and back to the *doddi haus* where they all stood.

Daniel straddled the front tire and held the bike still as he instructed Emma to sit on the seat. "I want to make sure it's a proper height for you, so sit on it and let me see if your feet can touch the ground."

Emma balanced on the seat and used her toes to steady herself.

"Perfect," Daniel said, moving to the back of the bike. Holding tightly to the seat, he instructed Emma to put her feet on the pedals.

"You're not going to let go, are you?" Emma asked in a nervous tone.

"Not until you're ready," Daniel reassured her as he jogged behind, trying to keep the bike level.

Marie sat on the top step and smiled as she watched Daniel hold the bike steady, not letting Emma fall.

Out of the corner of her eye, she watched as Amos pushed his tricycle out into the driveway and moved his tiny feet as fast as he could to catch up with his sister. A sense of contentment filled her. Looking over toward Nathan's porch, she noticed he had moved to the bottom of the stairs, protectively watching his children play. There was no doubt he loved his family, and other than the inconvenience she had caused, he looked relaxed. Turning her attention back to her own children, she watched as Daniel took his time assuring Emma he wasn't going to let her fall. For over an hour, she sat on the step, enjoying the laughter that filled the air. Rachel was riding in figure-eights as Amos followed. Emma continued to try to balance herself but wasn't getting any closer to doing it on her own. At one point Nathan even walked over to give her some pointers. Enjoying the merriment, Marie had to admit she didn't want the afternoon to end.

Just as Emma had stopped for the day and was pushing the bike back to the porch, they all heard the scrape of metal on metal, and Amos scream. Without hesitating, Marie raced across the driveway to where Amos lay in the dirt. His trike and Rachel's bike were tangled in a heap around them. Rachel stood and started to cry when she saw blood on her knee. Just as Marie reached Amos, Nathan was behind her, pulling Rachel's bike off the top of him. When the bike moved, the boy cried louder.

"Stop," Marie hollered. "It's his foot."

She pointed to the way his ankle angled away from his body. "I think it's broken," she said softly, so Amos wouldn't hear.

Nathan checked Amos over for other injuries and gently moved the twisted contraptions away from him. Marie lay on the ground, whispering calming words in the child's ear. From the corner of her eye she saw Emma lead Rachel away and into the house.

Daniel pulled up his truck and opened the passenger door. "It will be faster if I drive you to the emergency room than wait for an ambulance, if you think we can move him."

"I don't see anything other than his ankle," Nathan said. "I think it will be fine to pick him up."

Reaching for Amos, he was surprised when the boy held his arms out to Marie instead.

Looking over to Nathan, Marie said, "Before I pick him up, let's get a pillow to put his foot on."

With Amos still holding his arms out to her, she leaned in closer and reassured him she'd pick him up as soon as his *datt* returned with a pillow. She rubbed the side of his cheek and kissed his forehead, holding his face close to hers as they waited.

Within seconds Nathan returned and nestled the boy's foot in the confines of the pillow. Working together, Nathan lifted his leg as Marie wrapped her arms around his back and tucked his tiny head in the crook of her neck. Walking slowly to the truck, Marie slid across the front seat, holding tightly to the sobbing child. Positioning him on her lap, Nathan lifted his son's leg enough to scoot the pillow underneath it, resting his foot on the pillow. Without hesitating, Daniel put the truck in drive and headed in the direction of the hospital. Amos continued wailing, shaking his head back and forth most of the way to the hospital.

Amos had just started to calm down as they pulled under the overhead entrance of the Emergency Room. His sobs had changed to hiccups as he drifted to sleep in Marie's arms. Waiting for Nathan to push the door open, they moved in unison as they left the truck and carried him through the automatic doors. Nathan led them to a row of chairs in the waiting room and got them both settled before he checked in at the front desk.

Reaching over Amos's head for a tissue from the stand beside her, Marie wiped his nose and ran the back of her hand across his brow. Looking down at his angelic face, she couldn't help but confess to herself that he'd stolen a piece of her heart. She pushed his hair away from his eyes, and saw a single tear drop from her face to his cheek. Surprised at her own reaction to the pain of the child, she quickly wiped her face with the tissue she held in her hand.

Within a few minutes, Nathan sat beside her and Daniel came in from parking the truck and found a seat near them. Nathan leaned in and whispered that there were a few people in front of them and they would have to wait their turn.

"He's asleep," she replied in a hushed tone. "As long as we don't have to move him for a few minutes, I think we can keep him settled."

"Is he getting heavy? Do you want me to take him?"

"No, I think it's best we don't move him again until we have to."

Nathan took his hat off and laid it on the chair next to him.

They sat in silence for the next thirty minutes as they waited their turn. When Nathan heard his name called, he jumped up and directed the nurse to where he stood.

Seeing the angle of Amos's foot, the nurse said, "Let me get a gurney. He might be more comfortable if we lay him down."

"I think he'll stay calmer if you let her carry him," Nathan said quickly.

Marie had pulled up her hair and wore the long denim skirt she bought last week so it wasn't strange the nurse assumed she was the boy's mother, when she said, "Okay, Mom, let's move him carefully and try to keep him asleep for as long as we can."

Neither of them corrected the woman in blue scrubs. At that moment, Amos's comfort was more important than an awkward explanation neither of them wanted to make.

Following the nurse into the examination room, Marie laid Amos on the table. He immediately started to whimper when she removed her hold on him. Opening his eyes, he reached out for her as she pulled the chair near the head of the bed and laid her head near his cheek. Whispering in his ear, she wrapped her arm around his middle and tried to avert his attention from the doctor at the end of the table.

The doctor asked Nathan to explain what happened while he carefully looked over the boy's ankle. Amos winced in pain as the doctor slid his fingers under his foot to feel the underside of his ankle. Stopping before causing him any more pain, he motioned Nathan to follow him out of the room.

Marie watched as the doctor and Nathan left the room but immediately turned her attention back to Amos as he tried to move his head closer to Marie's shoulder. "I know, sweetie, you want me to pick you up, but you need to lie still for a little bit longer. The doctor's going to make you feel better real soon."

Rubbing her fingers along the side of his cheek, she started to softly hum in his ear, trying to lull him back to sleep. No sooner did he relax than Nathan came back in and whispered in her ear.

"He wants to get an X-ray. He's pretty sure they will need to set it before they cast it. He's calling in a pediatric orthopedic surgeon. He doesn't think he'll need surgery, but he wants the surgeon to read the X-ray to be sure."

Just as Nathan finished repeating what the doctor had told him, the nurse came in to take Amos to the X-ray department. Instantly stirring, he started to cry as soon as he saw the nurse. Leaning in closer to Marie, Nathan smiled down at him, shook his head, and said in a teasing tone. "If you wanted a new bike, all you had to do was ask. You didn't need to run into your *schwester* and bend your handlebars to get one."

"I can have a new bike?" Amos asked between hiccups.

"Maybe not a tricycle, but maybe you can learn to ride a two-wheeler along with Emma," Nathan said. "What do you think about that?"

Amos smiled and looked toward Marie. "I'm hungry. Can I have some ice cream when we get home?"

"You bet you can," she said. "Maybe we can talk *Datt* and Daniel into taking turns cranking the ice cream bucket. I saw one in the corner of the basement yesterday."

She barely finished her sentenced before Amos closed his eyes.

The nurse checked the needle she taped to the back of his hand and told them they would be taking him down to X-ray in a few minutes. She offered to bring Nathan a chair, and he declined. After they wheeled Amos from the room, Marie stood and shook her arm. It had fallen asleep from holding Amos so tightly. Without the child to care for, an uncomfortable silence filled the room.

"I should go update Daniel," she said quickly. "He's probably wondering what's going on."

Without waiting for his response, she left the room.

~~

Alone in the examination room, Nathan straddled the chair, crossed his arms over the back, and rested his head on his forearms. For the last two hours, he'd let adrenaline direct his actions. But now, he tried to relax in the quietness of the room. He was glad Marie had left. The antiseptic smell and the hospital sounds took him back to the day he sat by Suzy's bedside, watching her slowly slip away from him. The car that hit her buggy threw her into the road. Her head injuries were so bad there was no saving her. The trauma team was able to keep her alive long enough that he was able to come and say goodbye. His life changed forever that day, and here he was again, almost to the day he handed his *fraa* over to her heavenly father. As he sat with his eyes closed, he heard a small voice from somewhere in the depths of his soul whisper to him. *Fear not, for I am with you; be not dismayed, for I am your God: I will strengthen you, I will help you, I will uphold you with my righteous right hand.*

131

Just that morning, he had read the verse in Isaiah over and over again. He didn't think he had memorized it, but where else would it have come from? Trying to not make sense of the voice, he suddenly felt a peace about him. Lifting his head off his arms, he looked around the room, trying to see anything that would explain the instant change in the feel of the room. It was a warmth and calmness he hadn't felt in over a year.

Chapter 15 - Ice Cream

Marie stood at the kitchen sink, washing out the ice cream bucket while Nathan got Amos settled on a daybed in the corner of the room. It had been a long day, but Amos didn't forget about the promise of ice cream. With his ankle in a cast and propped up on a pillow, he was anxious for the creamy dessert.

Emma had warmed up the casserole they made yesterday, and everyone ate as soon as they got home. Rachel stood over her *datt,* waiting to sit by Amos and inspect his baby blue cast. Emma had seen to the scrape on Rachel's knee. All that was left to do was dote on her baby *bruder.*

Marie poured the mixture of sugar, cream, and vanilla into the canister and secured the paddle in place. "All it needs now is some muscle," she heard herself say.

No sooner had the words exited her mouth than Daniel appeared at the front door. "I have everything ready," he announced. "The ice is waiting, and I found a box of rock salt in the basement."

Handing Daniel the canister, Marie spoke quietly so only he could hear. "I'm not sure he'll stay awake as long as it's going to take to make it, but he'll get to enjoy it tomorrow."

Drying her hands on a kitchen towel, Marie turned and watched Rachel and Nathan make sure Amos had everything he needed. The ride home had been quiet, but there was something about Nathan's disposition that had changed. Nathan moved to let Rachel sit beside her *bruder* so they could look at a book together.

Walking out of the kitchen without saying a word, Nathan headed straight to his *mamm's* room. Rosie had already retired before they got home, but he was sure she'd want to be filled in about Amos.

Pulling a chair close to the temporary bed Daniel had made in the kitchen for Amos, Marie sat and watched Rachel. The girl brought Amos his favorite wooden toy and tucked his brown bear under the blanket beside him. She was the perfect little helper.

The minute Marie sat, Amos found her eyes. "I want to watch Daniel turn the ice cream," he said in a whining voice.

Marie patted his arm. "He can't do it in the house; the ice and salt will splash out," she lovingly explained. "He needs to do it out on the porch."

Watching his face turn to disappointment, she said, "How about when *Datt* gets done talking to *Mommi*, we ask him if you can sit on the porch for a little while?"

Rachel stood. "Can I help too?"

Taking the book from Rachel's hand, Marie said, "How about I sit with Amos for a few minutes, and you go ask Emma and Daniel if you can take a turn churning the ice cream."

Without hesitation, her tiny feet made their way across the polished wood floor and out to the porch. Her long braid and yellow dress barely made it through the door before it slammed behind her.

Opening the book Rachel left for him, Marie asked Amos if he would like her to read the story. Nodding his head and snuggling the bear under his chin, he made himself comfortable as Marie started to read.

~~

Nathan stood as the early evening shadows gathered in the room, watching how Marie tenderly cared for his son. Listening to her quietly read him a story, something stirred in him. A memory he had long forgotten. Suzy had been insistent that both *kinner* learn English as soon as they started talking. He never understood why she was so adamant about it, but here and especially today, when Amos needed the comfort of a woman, he was happy he didn't have a language barrier to contend with. Opening the screen door quietly, he joined Daniel, Emma, and Rachel on the porch.

"How's the ice cream coming?" he asked, relieving Rachel from her turn at the handle.

Emma was the first to answer. "It will be a while. I hope Amos will be able to stay awake long enough to enjoy it."

"Not so sure about that," Nathan said, "he's just about asleep now."

Adding more rock salt to the bucket, Emma replied, "He had quite a day. I'm sure sleep is what he needs. We can save some for him, and he can enjoy it tomorrow."

Nathan stopped long enough to add more ice. "If I know my son, it'll be the first thing he asks for the minute he opens his eyes."

Emma snickered and moved to take her turn.

Moving out of Emma's way, Nathan sat in one of the rockers and let Rachel crawl up on his lap.

"Let me see that scrape on your knee," he said, positioning his daughter on his lap.

"Emma fixed me up right good," she said.

"Looks like she did a fine job. I think we've had enough bike riding for a few days."

"But, *Datt*. Emma still needs to learn to ride. She was starting to get the hang of it, and we need to keep practicing."

"You're not going to do any riding until I fix those handlebars. You and Amos did a number on both bikes. How you got so tangled, I'll never know."

"Daniel straightened them out."

"He did, did he?"

"Yep, they're good as new. We have to keep practicing. Please, pretty please, *Datt,* can I keep showing Emma how to ride?"

"We'll talk about it tomorrow. For now, let's just worry about getting that ice cream made."

Knowing better than to push her *datt*, Rachel climbed off his knee and went to sit on the top step with Daniel.

For the next thirty minutes, they each took their turns churning the creamy mixture until it reached the perfect consistency.

Retrieving a quilt from the back of one of the rockers in the sitting room, Emma folded it in layers and wrapped it around the bucket. "I think it's just about ready. It needs to sit for another thirty minutes or so and freeze up more before we can dish it out. Rachel, how about I help you get your nightgown on while we wait?"

Nathan watched as Rachel followed Emma in the house. Turning to Daniel, he asked, "Feel like taking a walk through the stables with me? I want to check on Sir Philip. He sure is a nervous one, and he tends to get the whole barn in a ruckus if he isn't settled himself."

Daniel stood and followed him off the porch.

~~

Quietly as she could, Marie gathered enough bowls and spoons from the cupboard to carry to the porch. She wasn't sure if Nathan would leave Amos to sleep on the daybed or take him to his room, but for now, she would let him rest where he was. Lighting the stove like Emma had taught her, she filled the pot with water, added coffee to its basket and placed the enamel percolator on the heat. Adding four cups to the tray with the bowls, she sat at the table, waiting for the coffee to perk. She couldn't help but feel Amos had changed something in her. It had been so long since anyone needed her. Her heart swelled with a fondness for the boy she couldn't explain. It surprised her that the child would want her to comfort him instead of his father.

Looking around the dimly lit kitchen, Marie felt at peace. Where did that come from, she wondered. Just a week ago she sat in her shared cell agonizing over what her life would look like on the outside. And here, a week later, she was sitting somewhere she never would have dreamed of—inside an Amish kitchen taking care of another woman's child. What was it Rosie said? *The only way we know something is in God's plan is to compare it to His word.*

Startled by the chime of the clock, she listened as it rang eight times. The familiar sound flashed a memory of her mother to her mind. She could see the black veil she always wore on the back of her head, a symbol of her submission to God. Marie was haunted by the disappointment on her mother's face. When she chose not to follow her Mennonite upbringing, it put a wedge in their relationship that she never got a chance to fix. The heartache of how much she had disappointed her ate away at her like nothing else, even more

136

than not being able to help Jake. Looking back on things, they both were a mess. If only Jake's family would have accepted her, and if she would have listened to her mother, maybe things would have been different. Hearing the gurgle of the percolator, she shook the memories from her head and poured coffee into the cups on the tray.

Pushing the screened door open with her hip, Marie carried the tray to the porch. Emma, sitting in a chair close to the door, immediately stood and took the tray and laid it on the stand between the chairs.

"I figured the ice cream would be just about ready by now. I think I brought out everything we might need. Rachel, do you want sprinkles on yours?"

"Sprinkles, yum," the little girl replied. "I know where they are, I'll go get them."

"Be extra quiet; we don't want to wake your brother."

Watching as Rachel gently opened the screened door and tiptoed to the kitchen, Marie smiled at the little girl's eagerness to be quiet.

Emma shifted in her chair. "How are you? I wasn't sure how going to the hospital with Nathan would go."

Marie looked toward the barn to be certain Nathan wasn't in earshot before she answered. "Surprisingly, it went fairly well," she replied. "I sat with Daniel in the waiting room while they set his ankle and cast it. Amos asked for me as soon as he woke up, and Nathan was great about coming to get me. He barely said two words to me, but a part of me felt he was glad he didn't have to handle it on his own."

Emma smiled and kept silent as she picked up a cup off the tray.

Opening the door gently, Rachel came back on the porch carrying a small jar of rainbow sprinkles. Anxious to enjoy the dessert they all worked on, she lifted the edge of the quilt, hoping to get a peek inside. "Emma, do you think it's ready?"

"I'm pretty sure it is, but let's wait until Daniel and your *datt* make it back from the barn. As soon as you see them, you let me know, and I'll remove the quilt and take the cover off."

Moving to the step, Rachel sat resting her chin in her hands, waiting for any glimpse of them through the shadows.

"It's a beautiful evening, don't you think?" Emma asked, looking toward her mother.

Marie crossed her legs and picked up a cup before she answered. "We've been so busy this week we haven't had a chance to enjoy the warm evenings. It feels nice just sitting here, even if it was a stressful day."

Rachel quickly stood up. "They're coming. Can we have ice cream now?"

~~

Marie carried the tray of empty bowls and the rest of the ice cream to the kitchen while Nathan carried Amos upstairs. Leaving the dishes in the sink, she warmed up her coffee and went back to the porch. She wanted to be sure Amos didn't wake up and ask for her before she walked across the yard to go to bed. Nathan had lit the lamp in the front room that sat on the small table near the window. Its warm glow bounced light through the window and out onto the porch. Rocking in the white chair, she waited to hear any signs of Amos from the opened upstairs window. Deciding to stay and enjoy the peacefulness of the farm from Nathan's porch, she savored the last few sips of her coffee.

Lost in her own thoughts, she was startled when Nathan came out to the porch carrying his own mug.

Walking to the edge of the porch, he didn't look her way but said, "thank you for today."

"You're welcome," was all she said.

An awkward silence filled the air, which forced her to carry her cup to the kitchen and leave through the side door. Walking through the dark, she felt Nathan's eyes on her back but refused to look his way. His thank you wasn't much, but she hoped it was a start in him trusting her with his children.

~~

Nathan moved to the chair as he watched Marie make her way through the yard. A part of him was relieved she'd been there to help him with Amos, but the other part of him worried that the boy was becoming too attached to her. The last thing he could do was set the boy up for more disappointment. First Suzy and then Sarah. He wasn't sure either of his *kinner* could handle many more women in their lives leaving them. He hated to admit it, but it was time he started to look for a new *fraa*. He'd make it a point to talk to the Bishop next week. There had to be somebody in their neighboring church district who would be a good fit.

A lump formed in the back of his throat thinking about Suzy. There would never be anyone who could replace her, and for that matter, he knew he would never feel the same about any other woman. At one time he thought that person might be Sarah, but the Bishop took care of that for him. Love wasn't an option. This time marriage would be one of convenience and nothing else. Someone who would be kind to Amos and Rachel and take care of his *mamm*. There had to be someone who could handle those tasks and not expect anything from him in return. He didn't have any love to give. All he needed was a caregiver. Running the questions over in his head, he thought. *Can I find a woman who only wants to care for my family and not care about an intimate relationship? A woman who would commit herself to the kinner without asking for anything in return? I have to find someone and quickly. Before any of them get too attached to Marie.*

Looking out over the home he had built, Nathan suddenly felt alone. At least when Sarah was there she would join him on the porch, and it helped him fill the quiet time before he retired to his empty bed. Without realizing it, his mind went back to Marie. Slightly smiling, he remembered how she tenderly cared for Amos and her gentleness reading him a story. For a woman who had been separated from her own children for so long, he saw a softness in her that for certain she didn't see in herself. *It doesn't matter,* he thought. After he spoke to the Bishop, he was sure he'd let him release her from her duties. Especially if Bishop Shetler knew he was serious about finding them a new *mamm*.

~~

For the next few days, Nathan stayed as far from Marie as he could. Emma had done a great job teaching Marie all she needed to know to run an Amish household. Even Rachel took turns with Amos, bringing him toys and his coloring books and building blocks. Rosie ventured out to the sitting room throughout the day, more looking for conversation than anything else. Emma made it a point to leave Rosie's ointment regimen to Marie. Marie wouldn't admit it, but she had started to enjoy her quiet time with the older woman.

Picking up the tube of cream and heading to the sitting room, Marie pulled up a chair to Rosie's knee and unscrewed the cap. Putting a small dab on the back of her hand, she rubbed the cream into the silky skin of Rosie's crippled hands. One thing Marie had learned was Rosie didn't hold back. She said whatever was on her mind.

"So, tell me why you avoid touching people," Rosie asked curiously? "I've been watching you for two weeks now, and you avoid every form of human contact except with Amos and Rachel. And of course, putting this cream on my hands."

Marie didn't say a word and continued to work the menthol cream into Rosie's skin.

"You know I've heard stories about your husband," Rosie continued. "I know he drank a lot. Did he hurt you?"

With her last comment, Marie stopped and looked directly into Rosie's eyes. "How do you know about my late husband?"

"You're avoiding my question with another question," Rosie said in a stern but quiet tone. "Tell me what happened."

Screwing the cap back on the tube, Marie laid it on the stand beside Rosie's chair. "If I don't let anyone get close to me, I don't have to worry about someone using their hands to control me."

Pulling a tissue from the box to wipe her hands, she moved the chair back to its place and started to walk from the room.

"How can you think your children will harm you? You may not see it, but Emma is trying to reach you, and so is Daniel. They have suffered much as well, and if you expect them to have a loving relationship with you, you'll need to let them in."

Continuing to talk to her even as she left the room, Rosie called out. "He wasn't always like that, you know."

Stopping and turning in her tracks, Marie repeated the woman's words. "He wasn't always like that? How would you know what he was like? Did you know Jake Cooper?"

"No, I can't say I knew Jake Cooper."

Confused by Rosie's comment, Marie shook her head and continued to the kitchen. *"No, he wasn't always like that, but how would she know that anyways? For someone I'm trying to forget, why does his memory keep showing up?"*

Bracing her hands on the sink and thinking of Rosie's words, Marie noticed a part of her was angry that the old woman felt she had the right to tell her how to handle her children. Maybe she had some say with Amos and Rachel, but Daniel and Emma were her children, and she'd deal with them in her own way. It was going to take more than a couple of weeks to make up for years of lies Emma had been told and the disappointment Daniel had endured. All she could do was hope they would give her the time she needed to work things out in her own mind first.

From the other room, Rosie hollered. "I am the light of the world. Whoever follows me will not walk in darkness, but will have the light of life."

Sighing and turning on the spigot to drown out her words, Marie continued thinking to herself. *What is it with this woman and spouting off Bible verses to me? She can't really think a few words are going to change things.*

Chapter 16 – Livestock Auction

Just as Marie put the platter of warm pancakes in the center of the table, everyone settled into their chairs. Amos started to talk, but Nathan quickly quieted him until they had bowed their heads. As soon as he cleared his throat, Amos began again.

"Is today Auction Day?"

"It is, but I'm not sure you're up to maneuvering the arena."

"But you can carry me," Amos said in a hopeful voice.

"I have work to do while I'm there, and I won't have time to keep an eye on you. Not sure you can go with me today. How about we wait until you get that cast off and can get around a little better?"

Amos dropped his head in disappointment and pushed his cut-up pancake around on his plate.

Watching how restless Amos had been the last couple of days, Marie knew getting out of the house may be just what he needed. Not sure how Nathan would respond, she put her fork down and weighed her words carefully.

"Emma promised to make cookies with Rachel, and I've never been to a horse auction before. If you wouldn't mind, I could sit with Amos while you handled your business at the auction house."

"Can she, *Datt*? I'll be good and sit with her the whole time. You won't have to watch me for one minute."

How could he tell him no? Nathan knew the boy was going stir crazy not being able to go outside and play like he was used to. Looking over to Marie, he said, "I like to go early and watch the tack sale, and the horse auction doesn't start until early afternoon. We'll be there for quite some time. Are you sure you want to sit through that?"

"I'm sure. It will do me good to get out of the house, too. And like Amos said, you won't have to watch us for one minute."

Smiling in the direction of Amos, she watched as his appetite returned.

"I'll leave around ten." That was all Nathan said as he finished his breakfast.

A few minutes before ten, Amos and Marie sat on the top step of the porch waiting for Nathan to pull the carriage around to the front of the house. Before Marie had a chance to pick Amos up and carry him to the buggy, Nathan hopped down and met them at the stairs, picking Amos up in one swoop. Settling him on the back seat, he walked around to help Marie inside. When she refused to take his hand to help her up, he left her side and took his own place behind the reins. With only a click of his tongue, his horse instinctively guided the buggy in the direction of the road. Pulling off beside the picket fence lining the driveway, Nathan tipped his hat as he waited for the brown delivery truck to make its way past him and to the house.

"I don't remember ordering anything," he said, puzzled. "I wonder what he is delivering?"

Marie watched Nathan skillfully guide the buggy onto the busy highway that led to the Sugarcreek Livestock Auction at the edge of town. He had rolled open the windows in the buggy to let air in, but the morning sun was already beating on the black-top buggy, making it too warm for her. She couldn't figure out if the uneasiness in her stomach was from the fear of going out in public or being so close to Nathan. Without Daniel or Emma to filter the tension, she was left to find a way to do it herself. Turning in her seat to check on Amos, her knee bumped Nathan's thigh, and she instinctively moved closer to the door. Unlike Daniel's truck, where she could hug the passenger side door, the confines of the buggy left her no other choice but to sit close.

Knowing conversation wasn't going to come easy with Nathan, she turned her attention to Amos. "You know this is the first time I've ridden in a buggy?"

"Never, really?" Amos was surprised.

143

"Nope, never," she responded, looking over her shoulder. "This is my first."

"I like *Datt's* buggy," the boy said, turning in his seat to look out the open-air window. "Cars go too fast, and they hurt my *Mamm*."

Just then, a truck passed them so quick it rattled the inside. The horse jerked to the right.

"Whoa, boy!" Nathan said, gently pulling back on the reins to slow the horse down.

Startled by the swift movement, Marie watched as the horse followed Nathan's every command.

"That was close. Does that happen often?"

"This is Sir Philip, and he's still in training. He tends to get a bit jumpy around big trucks."

Pulling off to the side of the road, Nathan let a line of cars pass while he gave the horse a few minutes to rest. Exiting the buggy, Nathan walked to the front of the horse.

Amos leaned up in his seat. "It's okay, don't be scared. *Datt* is good with horses."

"I can see that. I guess we're lucky he knows just what to do."

Marie watched as Nathan rubbed Sir Philip's neck and whispered reassuring words near his head. The muscular black horse responded to his gentle touch. She couldn't help but notice Nathan's cold exterior softened when it came to his family and horses. Even the way he dealt with the stable hands spoke a great deal about his underlying character. Other than Sarah, with whom he was clearly upset, Marie realized she had been the only person to whom he was cold and distant. *I can't blame him. I've been dumped in his lap, and he's been given no other choice but to tolerate me.*

For the next twenty minutes, she watched as they made their way through the town she had once called home. Once they arrived at the auction, Nathan asked her if she minded holding Amos while he tethered the buggy to the fence. Letting her off where a dozen bicycles were parked, she picked the boy up from the back seat and waited for Nathan to move the buggy before walking toward the door. The smell of livestock filled her nose, Marie studied large letters painted on the front of the cinder block building. The group of young girls they passed on Buckeye Street walked by, their flip

144

flops slapping their heels, making their presence known. Their mint green dresses and white head coverings made a bright contrast to the dismal gray and white building.

It took Nathan only a few minutes to find his way back to them. Taking Amos from her arms, he walked through the doors and up the steps. Following on his heels, Marie stopped long enough to wait for him to find an empty bench. Sitting Amos on the seat between them, he nodded hello in the direction of a few men to his left and waited until Marie sat before sitting himself.

Looking out over the arena, Marie took note of very few English. The gray wooden benches were filled with men sporting suspenders and black hats. A few women were mixed in between, and most of them had three or four children surrounding them. Nathan's purple shirt and straw hat matched a half dozen other men around them. For some reason, she suddenly felt out of place. Her hair pulled back in a ponytail, along with her blue jeans and plaid shirt, stood out against the sea of solid colors and covered heads. The few English men she noticed sat intermixed with the Mennonite and Amish men in attendance. Anxiety crept up the back of her neck as she recognized the man who had paid a visit to Nathan early last week looking their way.

Patting Amos on the top of his head and taking out his wallet to hand Marie a twenty-dollar bill, he said, "I need to go talk to the Bishop, and then I am going to inspect the horses that will be going up for sale." He pointed to the Snack Bar at the back of the building. "They have ice cream if he wants a snack."

Taking the bill from his hand, Marie watched Nathan's long strides weave through the sea of blue and black to the Bishop. She noticed how the Bishop sat, with his back straight and arms crossed in front. The way he was surrounded by a group of men spoke more about his position in the community than anything else. Having overheard Sarah talk to Emma, Marie knew he had forced Nathan's hand in hiring her and sending Sarah back to Willow Springs. The whole thing made her leery of the man. How one man could hold so much authority over an entire community was beyond her.

Amos pulled on her shirt sleeve. "That's my friend, Jonah," he said, pointing to two children sitting a couple of rows down. "Hi, Jonah!" he hollered, waving excitedly.

The young boy turned when he heard his name, and his mother did the same. The woman's smile quickly faded when she faced them. The ribbons on her starched *kapp* whipped around her neck just as fast. She pulled her child close and whispered something in his ear. Neither of them turned again to acknowledge them.

"I wonder why Jonah didn't say hi to me?" Amos said in a questioning tone.

Embarrassed by the woman's reaction to her, Marie diverted Amos's attention to the men in the center of the arena.

"Looks like they're getting ready to start the auction. Do you think your *Datt* will buy anything today?

~~

Noticing the Bishop the minute they climbed the steps to the arena, Nathan wasted no time seeking his attention. The sooner he told him of his plans, the sooner he could release Marie. He couldn't chance Amos getting any more attached than he already had.

"Bishop Shetler, can I have a few words with you?"

Taking a seat on his free side, Nathan took his hat off and started to spin it in his hands.

"Nathan, I heard about Amos, and I've meant to stop and check in on the boy. Do I need to do a special collection to help pay his Emergency Room bill?" Knowing the answer would be no, the Bishop waited for him to answer before continuing.

Lack of money had never been an issue for Nathan Bouteright; however, the absence of a woman to care for his *kinner* was more concerning. Nathan shook his head. "No, there is no need for that. I can take care of the bill myself."

Keeping his arms crossed in front of him, the Bishop nodded his head in Marie's direction. "I see your new housekeeper is settling right in. I'm surprised you haven't convinced her to trade those jeans in for proper attire."

Surprised at his comment, Nathan looked towards Marie. "Her choice of clothing is none of my concern," he said quietly. "I'm not planning on her being around that long to make a difference."

The Bishop turned his body toward Nathan and hooked his fingers under his suspenders. "What makes you think she won't be around long?

"Because I plan on looking for a *fraa*. That is what I want to talk to you about. I would like you to start asking around in the neighboring church districts to see if there is an older woman who might be a good match for the *kinner* and my *mamm*. Someone who is still young enough to take care of my household but isn't necessarily looking for a traditional husband."

The Bishop waited a few minutes, choosing his words carefully. Crossing his arms back over his chest, he finally asked, "Why would you want to find a woman who wasn't looking for a loving relationship? You're only forty and plenty young enough to raise more *kinner* and live a long life with a loving *fraa*. That's just crazy talk, and I'll not hear of it."

Nathan felt his back stiffen. "You might have a lot of say in this community," he responded, his voice less than cordial, "but you're crossing the line if you think you have any say about whether I marry for love or convenience."

The Bishop didn't answer. He stared ahead, pretending to be interested in what the auctioneer was rattling off.

Nathan didn't get angry at too many things, but the Bishop's comment made the hair stand up on the back of his neck. How was he going to convince him he had no desire to fall in love again? Putting his hat back on his head, he placed his hands on his knees. "I'll let you think on my request and ask you again in a few days if you've found anyone."

Without waiting for a response, he stood and headed back to where he had left Marie and Amos. Looking up to find them in the crowd, he noticed they were not in the same place where he'd left them. Figuring she'd taken him to get ice cream, he made his way to the Snack Bar. At the doorway, he looked around the line of people trying to find any sign of them. Turning to focus on what the auctioneer was pointing to, he pulled the numbered paddle from his back pocket, took a seat and started to bid on the items he came for.

After the items he was interested in had all been bid on, Nathan focused his attention back to looking for Marie and Amos. From across the room he saw her standing near the windows at the top of the benches, rocking Amos from side to side in her arms. Her back was turned from the crowd, but the brown-haired boy she held in her arms was snuggled in close. Even though the child was only four, his long legs and heavy cast would be a strain for anyone for any length of time. Before he had a chance to move in her direction, he heard three women from his church district sitting directly in front of him. Not caring to quiet their conversation they nodded their heads in Marie's direction.

"There's the woman who's taking care of Susan and Nathan's *kinner*. I heard she just got out of prison."

Sitting on the edge of his seat, knowing the women didn't know he was behind them, Nathan leaned in closer.

"Oh, help. I can't even imagine why the Bishop would allow such a thing. And those poor *kinner*, losing their *mamm* and then being forced to be looked after by such a woman. Well, I never."

Standing long enough to let his pant legs fall, he thought. *What right do they have to judge who I hire to take care of my family?* It was one thing to feel Marie wasn't the right person for the job, but to hear it from his neighbors. In an instant he leaned between the women and spoke. "One rotten apple corrupts all those that lie near it."

All three women gasped as Nathan towered over them.

Not waiting for any apologies, he turned and made his way to where Marie held Amos. Reaching out for the sleeping boy, he sat on the top row, moving over to give Marie enough room to sit beside him.

It didn't take Nathan but a minute to notice how the families around them scattered in their presence. Glancing over to catch Marie's reaction, he waited to see how she'd respond. Sitting up straight, she was focused on the activity in the center of the room. She didn't appear to notice the whispers and stares she was attracting.

Disgusted by the reaction of those he considered his friends, Nathan couldn't help but chastise himself for doing the same thing. Moving his attention back to the chant of the auctioneer, the sale suddenly lost its appeal. Repositioning Amos in his arms, he stood and started toward the stairs at the back of the arena. Looking over his shoulder only briefly to see Marie had followed him, he wasted no time making his way outside. At the buggy he didn't say a word, laying Amos across the back seat and going to Sir Philip to untie the reins. Waiting until Marie had caught up to him and climbed on the seat beside him, he directed the horse to make a circle and head back through town toward home.

Unsure if she should say anything, Marie waited until she was confident they were out of the heavy traffic before she spoke.

"It's a small town, and people talk."

Quick to respond, he said, "Even so, who I employ is none of their business. I didn't see any of those women stepping up to come and help me with the *kinner.*"

"Nathan, it's okay. I can deal with it. If you'd rather I not be in public with you or the children, I'll understand. I can always send Emma with you if need be. At least she wouldn't be scrutinized as much.

She waited for him to answer, but when enough time had passed and it was clear he wasn't going to, she changed the subject.

"I was surprised Amos fell asleep. He was so excited to come."

Nathan stopped the buggy, waiting for the traffic light to change. "He didn't sleep well last night," he said, looking back at his son. "He woke up a few times, complaining his foot was itchy. I wasn't sure what to do, so I woke up *Mamm,* and she suggested I use one of her knitting needles to scratch it. It worked, and he fell back to sleep."

Marie also turned to look over the seat. "Hopefully, it will heal quickly, and he won't have to wear that heavy cast for the full six weeks. What a way to spend the last months of summer."

Letting silence fall between them, Marie enjoyed the hypnotic clip-clop of Sir Philip's hooves on the paved highway. Happy to leave the prying eyes of Sugarcreek behind, she was anxious to return to the peacefulness of Nathan's home.

Chapter 17 - A Letter from Home

The smell of a summer rain woke Marie way before the alarm went off. A cool breeze filled the room, and she'd spent a few minutes enjoying it before getting up to start her day. The August heat had been unbearable, especially without the comfort of air conditioning. Anxious to get to Nathan's to start breakfast, she quietly grabbed her clothes off the end of the bed and left without waking Emma.

In the dim morning light, she glanced at her daughter's sleeping form. She knew she'd have to answer the questions she'd been asking about her father. She was well aware of the heaviness in the air. How could she think she could form a bond with either of her children in just a couple of weeks? Maybe she was expecting too much from both of them. Or perhaps they were expecting more from her than she was able to give. When she was young, being a mother came naturally. Even protecting them both from Jake's drunken rages became easy. But being a mother to older children was a challenge she hadn't considered. It was apparent she related better to Amos and Rachel.

Standing on the porch waiting for a slight break in the rain, Marie couldn't help but wonder if letting Daniel bring her here was the right thing to do.

~~

Emma heard the screen door shut and waited to make sure her mother had left the house before getting up. Typically she welcomed a summer shower, but this morning it only added to her blue mood. She felt no closer to getting Marie to open up than she was to finding information about her birth father. Making her way to the kitchen, she put water on for tea and sat at the table. In no hurry to help her mother with breakfast, she sat in the stillness of the room, wondering what *Gott* wanted her to do. Turning the wick up on the lamp over the table to light the room, she pulled her *mamm's* letter from her apron pocket and placed it on the table. Filling a mug with hot water and adding a mint tea bag, she let the herbal smell fill her nose. Dunking the tea bag up and down a few times, she let it seep as she ran her fingers over her *mamm's* familiar handwriting. Opening the envelope, she smiled as she read the first few lines.

Wednesday, August 23, 2017

My Dearest Emma,

The weather has been brutally hot this past week, but your datt says he feels rain in the forecast. You know how he has a sixth sense about the weather and frequently gets it right. Your schwesters say the garden could use some rain, so I hope he's correct. Rebecca and Anna have been busy washing and dyeing fleece, and by the looks of it, they have a winter's worth of fiber to spin.

I'm still feeling a bit under the weather. Datt made me make an appointment with the doctor. I couldn't get in to see him until next week, but hopefully, he can get to the bottom of why I can't shake this bug. The girls have been great about doing my chores, and I'm grateful for their willingness to help. It's hard to sit back and watch them, but I'm feeling so very weak these days. I feel blessed that Gott surrounded me with a caring family.

Ruth and Katie stopped by this morning and brought over a couple loaves of bread and an apple pie. Katie is missing you and was asking when I thought you might be back. She told me to tell you that she received another standing order from the Apple Blossom Inn. By the sounds of it, her budding bakery business is taking off. I bet you'll have your hands full helping her when you return.

Please don't take that as I'm rushing you home, I'm not. I understand your need to get to know your birth family and don't

152

want to stand in your way of what you feel you need to do. I pray you get the answers you need, and Gott will show you the path he wants you to take. Even your datt knows this is what you have to do.

Ruth said she saw Sarah Mast in town yesterday, and she mentioned she'd spent a little bit of time with you before she left. Matthew has been in a good mood for the last few days, and I'm wondering if Sarah had anything to do with that. Not sure what's going on there, but I'm sure I'll find out when I'm supposed to know. He's been busy fencing in new pasture space for a project he and your Datt have been talking about. Not sure what that's all about either, but again I'll find out in time.

I hope you are doing well, and I just wanted to let you know that we love and miss you. I pray that whatever you decide, you'll always let your datt and me be a part of your life. Looking back over the last sixteen years, I suppose we had more than one time when we could have shared things with you, but your datt always felt so strongly about waiting. Please don't be angry with him and know that he loves you even though he's had a hard time showing you lately.

I'm getting tired and want to go lie down but want to share this one last thing with you. I believe that Gott has a purpose for each of us, and if we are faithful enough to follow where the Spirit leads us, He will guide us through the life He's planned for us. I know how hard it is to trust Him in everything we do, but I have learned not to question the why, but look for what he's trying to teach me through the process.

Look for what He's trying to do through you, Emma, and not so much at the reason He placed you where he did. It's not by some small miracle Daniel moved to Willow Springs and became friends with Matthew. How was it Daniel happened to know Nathan Bouteright, who happened to be in the same church district as Anna Mae? Too many coincidences to not be part of Gott's bigger plan. It amazes me when I sit back and watch how He orchestrated every moving part for it all to come together in His perfect timing. This is not the work of your Datt, or me, or even Marie; this is all part of Gott's plan He had for you.

Out of all my girls, you're the one who is most equipped to handle this difficult situation. Don't fret about your datt, he's coming around and by the time, God-willing you come home, all will be well.

All my love,

Mamm

Folding the letter and placing it back in its envelope, Emma tucked it back in her pocket and picked up the mug of tea. Carrying it to the door, she sipped the warm liquid as she watched the rain flow off the porch roof. Thinking of *Mamm's* words, she had been doing exactly what she had said. For the last few days, she'd been moping around trying to figure out why *Gott* had sent her there. Feeling she wasn't able to connect with Marie yet was unnerving. *Gott, I want to open my eyes to you. What is it you are trying to show me? If you put me in this exact place in your exact time, then help me be open to what you want me to do.*

Stepping out on the porch, she remembered the box that had been delivered yesterday. It sat near the door with Marie's name and Nathan's address clearly printed on it. She wondered why her mother hadn't brought it inside. Too big for her to carry across the yard, she'd have to ask Daniel to get it after breakfast.

Noticing the rain had let up for a few minutes, Emma took it as her chance to make it across the driveway without getting totally soaked. Forgoing shoes, she ran through the puddles and up the front steps to Nathan's house. Rachel was waiting for her just inside the door. She handed her a kitchen towel to dry her face.

"We were waiting for you," the child said. "Marie said you were still sleeping and I wanted to go wake you up, but Marie told me I should let you be."

"I was a sleepyhead, but I'm here now," Emma responded. "Let's go help Marie with breakfast before the others come in from the barn. I'm sure they'll be extra hungry this morning since it's not so hot."

Guiding the girl to the kitchen, Emma was surprised her mother had most of the table set and breakfast ready.

"What can I help you with?" Emma asked, moving to the silverware drawer.

"I made a French toast casserole, and it needs to come out in about five minutes. I'm going to see if Rosie needs my help. Amos is in the bathroom. Can you help him when he calls?"

Without waiting for Emma to answer, Marie walked through the sitting room and knocked softly on Rosie's door.

"Rosie, are you up? Do you need my help this morning?"

Not hearing an answer, she gently turned the knob. Adjusting her eyes to the still-dark room, Marie hollered quickly for Emma. Rosie was lying on the floor. Snapping the green shade to filter light into the room, she hollered again to get Emma's attention. Dropping to her knees, she felt for a pulse and leaned in close, calling her name.

Finally hearing Emma, Marie said, "Go get Nathan. It looks like she fell trying to get out of bed. I'm not sure if she's hurt, but quickly go get him."

Hearing the slam of the screen door and feeling Rachel at her side, she turned to the little girl.

"It looks like *Mommi* fell out of bed. Can you be a big sister and go help Amos in the bathroom? I hear him calling."

Making sure Rachel had left the room before she turned her attention back to Rosie, she gently ran her hand on the back of her head to make sure she wasn't bleeding. When she didn't feel a bump or anything wet, she went back to softly shaking her. Rosie's pulse was steady, and her chest rose and fell with breaths. Marie could see no visible injuries and wasn't sure why she wasn't responding to her voice. Grabbing a pillow off the bed, she placed it under her head as she waited for Nathan.

"Rosie, can you hear me? You need to wake up now."

Opening her eyes, Rosie looked up at Marie and said, "I can hear you just fine."

"Are you hurt? Don't move. Nathan and Daniel will be here any minute."

"I don't feel any pain anywhere. I heard you moving around in the kitchen, and when I tried to get up, I slipped and fell. I knew you'd be coming in to check on me and decided I would just wait. I must have fallen back to sleep. Quit fussing over me and help me up."

155

"You're not going to get up until Nathan gets here."

With that, she heard his heavy steps and long strides come up the front steps. Not moving from Rosie's side, Marie waited until Nathan made his way to his *mamm*'s room.

"What happened?" Nathan asked as he came through the door.

"She said she slipped and decided to just wait for me to come to get her up. She says she must have fallen back asleep, but I don't want her to move until you check her over real good."

Nathan moved to Rosie's feet, picking up each leg and moving it, making sure there was no pain or sign of anything out of place.

"Are you hurting anywhere?"

In a snippy tone, Rosie said, "Would you two stop? I told you I'm fine. I'm not hurt; I decided to stay put, and I knew one of you would find me eventually. And you did. Now help me up off the floor before I catch a cold."

Rosie looked over her son's shoulder toward Emma and Daniel standing in the doorway. "Who's watching breakfast?" she snapped. "I smell something burning."

"Oh, help! The casserole," Emma shouted as she took off, running toward the kitchen.

Seeing Marie and Nathan had Rosie under control, Daniel followed Emma.

After Nathan was sure she hadn't broken anything, he directed Marie to her side so they both could lift her in unison off the floor and back to her bed. Pushing Nathan's hand away from her side and pointing to the door, Rosie said, "She can help me from here. You go about your business. We'll be out for breakfast as soon as I get dressed."

Nathan looked at Marie. "I guess I've been excused. Are you sure you've got this?"

"I'm good. If you can go check on Amos, that would be great. I left him in the bathroom, and I sent Rachel to check on him. We'll be out in a few minutes."

"Just holler if you need me," Nathan said, pulling the door shut behind him.

Marie took the purple dress off the hook by the door and stood in front of Rosie. "You gave us quite a scare. How about from now on you wait for me to come to help you before you try to get out of bed?"

"I'll do that if you promise to get me up as soon as you get here in the morning. I might not be much help, but I hate being cooped up in this room so much."

Helping her pull the white cotton nightgown up over her head, Marie said, "It's a deal. I didn't want to disturb you, but now that I know you'd rather be out where we are, I'll make a point to help you get dressed before I start breakfast."

Helping her put her arms through the sleeves of her dress, Marie pinned the cape closed with straight pins just like Emma showed her. Taking the brush off the dresser, she ran it through Rosie's waist-length white hair and twisted it in a bun like she had seen her own mother do for years. Adding a hairnet over the bun, she pinned the starched white kapp in place and stood back to see if she had secured it in place evenly.

Placing her hand under her elbow, Marie helped Rosie stand. Letting the older woman lean on her as they made their way to the kitchen, she made a mental note to talk to Nathan about a wheelchair. The wooden floors and lack of furniture would make it safer for Rosie to get around, and they wouldn't have to worry about her slipping and falling as much.

~~

After getting Rosie settled and Amos down for a nap, Marie took a break and retreated to the front porch. The rain had all but stopped, and the sun was starting to peek through the clouds. Emma had taken Rachel with her to visit her aunt, and Daniel and the men were busy working with a few horses in the corral beside the barn. The box that Emma had Daniel carry over after breakfast still sat near the rocking chair, unopened.

Turning the box around looking for any signs on who may have sent it, she took the utility knife she found in the kitchen drawer and made a slice through the transparent tape that kept its contents a secret.

Opening the lid, she pulled away a layer of white tissue paper to reveal the quilt that once covered the bed she and Jake had shared. The sight of it made her gasp at the memories it stirred. The quilt had made its way to their tiny apartment in almost the same manner – in a cardboard box with no return address. The familiar gray double wedding ring pattern looked identical to the one she had seen on Nathan's bed, except the fabric that made up the center star was baby blue. Pulling the quilt from the box, Marie noticed a small lily, embroidered in white on the corner. She had forgotten about that. She was sure it was some sort of identification mark added by the quilter, but they never did figure it out.

Without going through the rest of the box, she carried it inside and headed upstairs to Nathan's bedroom. A part of her felt she was invading his private space, but she just had to compare the two quilts more closely. Placing the folded quilt on top of his bed, she compared the stitches and pattern to compare its similarity. If she didn't know better she could swear both quilts were made by the same person. Pulling each corner up and flipping it over to its backside, Marie looked for a lily. Her stomach flipped when on the last edge she saw it. The same small white lily embroidered into the exact spot as the one on her quilt. How could she ask Nathan about it without him knowing she'd been in his room? Tucking the quilt in around the bed just as she had found it, she picked up hers and headed back to the porch.

No sooner had she put it back in the box when Nathan walked up the stairs.

"I need to go into town and wanted to see if you needed anything before I left," he said. "I won't be long and should be back before supper."

Marie closed the lid of the box and stood. "We do need a few things. Do you have a few minutes? I could make a list."

Acting as if he was trying to decide whether he wanted to wait for a list or not, Nathan looked at her intently. "Is Amos still sleeping?"

"He is, but he should be waking up any time now."

"How about you just go with me? That would probably be best. I can wait until Amos wakes up."

Marie didn't think she could deal with being seen with him. "Are you sure?" she asked. "You know the reaction you'll get when you're seen with me again. I could make a quick list, and you can stop and pick up Emma and Rachel at the Troyers' on your way by. I'm sure Emma won't mind shopping while you run your errands."

Nathan turned back to the barn. "Just come get me when he wakes up," he said over his shoulder. After a few steps, he stopped and turned back toward her. "People are just going to have to get used to how things are."

Watching him walk away, she wasn't sure if that meant he expected her to go with him or not, but she'd figure it out after Amos woke from his nap.

Chapter 18 - Gott's Plan

Insisting he sit between Nathan and Marie on the way into Sugarcreek, Amos made sure there wouldn't be any uncomfortable bouts of silence. His little four-year-old mind was working a mile a minute, asking any and every question he could think of. Admiring the way Nathan calmly repeated the same answer multiple times without once getting frustrated, Marie enjoyed the banter they had with one another.

Slowing down just in time to direct his horse to pull into the bulk foods store at the edge of town, Nathan hopped out and tethered the buggy to the white fence at the front of the parking lot. Walking around to her side of the buggy, she handed Amos out to him.

"You sure are giving your ole' *Datt* a workout with all this carrying," Nathan told his son. "When we go back to the doctor next week, we're going to have to see about a walking cast. At least then, you can get around by yourself a good bit."

"But I like you carrying me," Amos said. "I can see better up here."

"I'm sure you can, but you're getting too heavy. Especially for Marie and Emma."

Walking ahead and through the doors, Marie grabbed a cart. She stopped close enough so Nathan could sit the boy down inside.

"There you go, almost as good as being carried, for sure and certain," Nathan said, pushing the cart ahead to follow Marie.

Pulling her list from her back pocket, Marie stopped long enough to get the lay of the store and to figure out which way would lead her to the baking aisle. Stopping at the row of spices, Marie lost herself in the array of choices. Knowing the store was filled with

160

Saturday shoppers, she tried to avoid looking anyone directly in the eye. The sooner she got what they needed, the sooner they could get back. It didn't take much to see flashes of purple, blue and black at every turn for her to realize the store was filled with Nathan's neighbors. Turning to add her selection to the cart, she saw Nathan nod in the direction of someone walking their way.

"Looks like the Bishop has something on his mind," Nathan said in a low voice.

Tipping his hat in Nathan's direction, the older gentleman stopped at the end of their cart.

"Fine day to be out and about, ain't so?" He reached inside the cart and patted the top of Amos's head. "How's that ankle doing, young man?"

Amos looked to his *datt* as if to ask if it was all right to respond. He waited for Nathan to nod his head before he answered.

"Good," the boy responded. "Marie said she'd make me more ice cream this week if I were good."

"She did, did she," the Bishop said, looking in Marie's direction. "I bet homemade ice cream would fix just about anything."

Turning his attention to Nathan, he asked, "I suspect I'll see you both at church tomorrow?"

Marie's stomach spun. "I'm not so sure that would be a good idea," she interrupted. "I think I've caused enough upheaval around here. I don't need to put Nathan and his family through any more."

Cocking his eyebrow, the Bishop looked at Nathan. "You haven't explained to her the stipulations of working for you yet?"

"No, but I think this situation is a little different."

The Bishop's friendly tone became stern. "I'd say you've made it quite well known that all of your employees attend Sunday service. This is no exception."

A heaviness filled the air as they stood unmoving, saying nothing. Marie watched as the two men exchanged glances. She could see the frustration etched on Nathan's forehead. The Bishop wasn't about to back down from his stand.

Taking a deep breath, Marie exhaled. "Nathan and I will talk about it, but not here in front of the boy if you don't mind."

The awkwardness was broken when a small woman walked up behind them. "Melvin, there you are. I was looking for you."

Taking the bag of sugar from her hand, the Bishop said, "I hadn't gone far and never too far to hear you call for me."

The Bishop looked Marie's way and moved back so his wife could be properly introduced. "Lilian, this is Marie Cooper. She is helping Nathan care for his *kinner* now that Sarah has gone back to Willow Springs. I was just inviting her to come to church tomorrow."

Marie had been around Nathan long enough to sense him stiffen as he listened to the Bishop's words. There was something in the way he looked at the older man that spoke of respect for his authority, but a challenge to his will as well.

Sensing a familiarity with the woman's maroon dress and neatly parted silver hair, Marie felt a shiver shoot up her neck. Smiling in Lilian's direction, she was cordial in her hello. When she looked Lilian in her eye, the woman instantly dropped her head and turned her attention back to her husband.

"Melvin, if you're done here, can we get going? I need to get these cookies made for the fellowship meal tomorrow."

The Bishop looked in Nathan's direction. "We'll talk more tomorrow," he promised. Turning to Marie, he added, "I hope to see you as well."

Marie glanced over at Nathan. She could tell by his furrowed brow he wasn't too happy with the exchange.

Without even thinking, Marie blurted, "What was that all about, and why is he so adamant I come to church?"

Nathan pushed the cart forward. "We can talk about it later."

After gathering the last few items on her list, Marie picked up Amos from the cart and waited for Nathan to pay and collect the filled bags. Following him out the door, she couldn't help but admire the calm manner in which he handled the Bishop. He had gotten quiet again, and she knew that typically meant he was in deep thought about something. Jake, on the other hand, had a short fuse, completely the opposite of Nathan. After putting the bags in the back

162

of the buggy, Nathan took Amos and waited for her to climb in before handing the boy back to her.

Once they had returned home, Nathan put the groceries on the table and immediately retreated to the barn. Marie helped Amos to the corner of the porch where he left his wooden toys.

"I'm going to go check on *Mommi,*" she told him. "I'll bring you out a snack when I'm done."

Amos picked up the polished hand-carved horse. "Are you going with us tomorrow?"

Marie patted the top of his head as she stood to leave. "I'm sure your *datt* and I will talk about it."

~~

As she started putting the groceries away, Marie found herself thinking about Lilian Shetler. What was it about the woman? The feeling she had met her before played over and over in her mind. Her mother had many Amish friends. It wouldn't be unlikely that she'd met her before. The Mennonite Church she attended as a child often was filled with Amish families visiting on their off Sundays.

Finding a place for all the groceries, Marie's thoughts returned to the box on the porch. Curious about what else it held, she picked up the new tube of ointment and headed to Rosie's room.

Knocking lightly on the door before opening it, she looked inside to see Rosie sitting in the chair by the window that overlooked the porch. The room smelled of menthol, and the large maple tree in the front yard kept the room shaded from the afternoon sun. Rosie was chatting with Amos, who sat outside her open window.

Looking to Marie, Rosie said, "I hear you're going to worship with us in the morning."

Marie knelt in front of Rosie's chair. "It's been a long time since I've been to church, and I'm not so sure it's a good idea," she said, squeezing a dot of cream over Rosie's knuckles. "It's not like I'd understand what's being preached anyways. Can't say I'd understand much High German."

She rubbed the cream in and braced herself for a lecture.

"Nathan has been known to hire English stable boys, and the ministers often repeat some of the key points of their sermons in English," Rosie pronounced. "I think it would do you good."

Marie felt herself stiffen. "How can subjecting you and Nathan to the stares and whispers of your neighbors be a good thing?" she retorted. "It's one thing to work for him, but it's a whole other thing being around people who will never accept me. It doesn't take a mind reader to know this community would rather I just go away."

She sat on the floor to rub ointment on Rosie's ankles. Looking up, she saw Rosie's slight smile.

"I surely hope you don't find this funny," Marie snipped. "I've put Nathan and my kids through enough just being here. I shouldn't have let Daniel bring me back to this town. If I had any other choice, I wouldn't have come back to Sugarcreek. This town will never welcome me."

Reaching over to lift Marie's hands up with her knotted fingers, Rosie held them and looked her in the eyes. "Child, you have it all wrong."

Marie tried to pull her hands away, but gave in when Rosie made it clear she wasn't letting go. "I see how Nathan looks at me," she said. "It's pretty hard for him to hide his distrust. And you didn't see how we were treated yesterday at the auction. It was pretty obvious that me being here and especially in Nathan's house is causing a stir."

Rosie continued looking directly in Marie's eyes. "Most people are just curious. Don't let a few prying eyes keep you from holding your head high. Those people don't know the whole story, and neither does Nathan. It's time you share it with him. I know my son, and what he's struggling with right now is not your past. It's letting his *fraa* go and allowing his *kinner* to get close to anyone again. Bishop Shetler was right to send Sarah home. Nathan was getting too comfortable with her here. It's time for him to move on, and he wasn't doing that with her around."

Pulling her hands from Rosie's grasp, Marie sat back on her heels and shook her head. "Wait a minute. How do you know there's more to my story, and did you say the Bishop's last name was Shetler?"

"I've said more than I should've. Now, help me to bed. I'd like to lie down for a bit before supper."

Marie could tell by Rosie's tone she wasn't going to get any explanations from her. Standing to help her walk across the room, she was consumed with the questions running through her head. *Shetler was a common name in Sugarcreek. Could it be?*

After getting Rosie to bed, she asked, "You're not going to tell me how you know about my past, are you?"

"It's not my story to tell, and you'll put the pieces together soon enough," the old woman said. "Now talk to Nathan. He needs to hear the whole story. And for people in this community, it's none of their business what you did or didn't do. *Gott* knows, and that is all that matters."

Marie headed toward the door, stopping when Rosie spoke.

"If you open your eyes and see how *Gott* placed you here for a reason, you'll understand that every event in your life had a purpose — which ultimately led you back to Sugarcreek. Look how easily Emma and Daniel accepted you back in their lives. Emma was raised by Amish parents, who taught her the true value of forgiveness. And look at Daniel. From what I hear he didn't have the best childhood. But he was adopted by Christian parents, who taught him the same values. Your children have accepted you for who you are and have forgiven you for the part you've played in their lives. It's time you forgive yourself and move on. Open your eyes. *Gott* has laid out his plan for you, but you're so consumed with your own self-pity you don't see it. If these old eyes can see it as clear as day, you should too."

Standing in the doorway without looking back, Marie waited for Rosie to finish before she closed the door and headed outside.

Walking to the edge of the porch, Marie closed her eyes and held her face up to the sun. She couldn't help but wonder why Rosie's words got under her skin so much. More importantly, how on earth did she know anything about her other than what Daniel had told them? Glancing over to Amos, who still played at the far end of the porch, she noticed the box still sat by the rocking chair near the door. Sitting in the chair and pulling it closer, she opened it, hoping there was something inside that would tell her who sent it. Before she had a chance to look inside, Rachel and Emma walked up the stairs.

Rachel ran to her and placed a brown paper sack in her lap. "Emma let me climb the apple tree in Anna Mae's yard to pick apples," she said excitedly. "Look how many we got!"

"Oh, my, I guess you and Emma need to make something for dessert then."

"Yep, we decided we'd make apple crisp. Doesn't that sound good?"

"It sure does. How about you go play with Amos for a few minutes? I want to talk to Emma."

Rachel turned to Emma. "You won't make it without me, right?"

Reassuring her she wouldn't, Emma pulled a chair closer to Marie. "I promise."

Emma waited for Rachel to get out of earshot. "Is something the matter?"

"No, not really. Nathan and I ran into the Bishop and his wife at the bulk food store today." Bracing both hands on the arms of the chair, Marie took a deep breath. "That's it," she said, almost gasping. "I knew I'd seen that woman before. She's your father's mother."

Startled by her mother's instant reaction, Emma asked, "What are you talking about? What woman? Who is my father's mother?"

"The Bishop's wife, Lilian."

"You mean Bishop Shetler?"

Marie leaned in closer to Emma, trying to hush her. "Shh … Rosie's window is open."

"How can that be? I thought you didn't know anything about his family."

"I don't know much and what I did know, I'm sure I've forgotten. But I do remember his birth name was Shetler, and I remember Lilian was the woman your father took me to meet when we got pregnant with Daniel."

"Are you sure? There are lots of families in the area with the last name Shetler."

"I didn't know his last name until Rosie mentioned it a few minutes ago. I didn't understand why he seems so interested in me, but I suspect he knows who I am. What do you know about him?"

"Not much. I've only just met him, but I have to say from the first time I talked to him, I got the feeling he knew more than he was letting on. Daniel said the same thing, but we could never pinpoint it. Here comes Daniel – let's ask him."

Taking the front steps two at a time, Daniel stopped in front of them. "Nathan asked me to come tell you we need to go fix a fence in the back pasture. He wants you to hold off supper for an hour or so if it's not too much trouble."

"Okay, no problem. Before you go, let me ask you something."

"Sure." Daniel leaned back on the porch railing.

Sitting up straighter in her chair, Marie asked, "What do you know about Bishop Shetler's family?"

"A little. He makes furniture, and his wife runs Lily's Quilt Shop in town. If I remember right, Rosie and Lilian are good friends. You might want to ask Rosie; she might know more about them than I do. I do know there is a mess of them. Ride up and down any of the back roads around here and you'll see that name on a good number of mailboxes."

Marie leaned back in her chair. "I'm sure Rosie knows more than she's letting on, and I plan on getting to the bottom of it."

Puzzled, Daniel asked, "What am I missing?"

"I was just telling Emma that we ran into the Bishop and his wife in town today, and he was insistent I go to church tomorrow. When he introduced me to his wife she could hardly look at me, and I thought it was because I was English, but now when I look back and remember it's because we've already met. Your father took me to see her when I was pregnant with you."

"Why would he take you to see her?"

"Because she's your father's mother."

"No way! That would make Bishop Shetler our grandfather."

Crossing his arms over his chest, Daniel cocked his head to the side. "Things are making sense now. I never understood why he went out of his way to speak to me like he did. He never did that to any other stable hands. I just thought he liked me better. But, he knows, right? He knows I'm his grandson. Why else would he welcome an Englisher into the folds of his community so easily?"

Emma interrupted him when she remembered something her aunt said. "Anna Mae told me that my Uncle Walter and my *datt* spent a lot of time with Bishop Shetler right after I was born. She never knew what they talked about, but she thought the Bishop was the one who suggested taking me back to Willow Springs."

Laying her hand on her mother's arm, Emma's voice became tender. "Momma, do you think he knew who we were all along?"

Marie looked down at her daughter's hand. For the first time she didn't want to pull away. Taking her free hand, she covered her daughter's touch. "I'm sure of it. I think your grandfather had a big part to play in keeping you safe. I think it's time he answers some questions from us. Maybe I will go to church tomorrow and see if I can't get him to talk to us. It's time this big family secret comes out in the open."

Daniel looked at Emma and then back to his mother. "I know you want to talk to him, but it's highly unlikely he'll talk to you at church," he said. "I think it's time we tell Nathan what we suspect and let him invite the Bishop here to talk to us. It's going to be hard enough on you going to worship tomorrow. The last thing you need is to bring more attention to the situation by being seen talking to him by yourself. Trust me on this one. It would be better to go through Nathan."

Marie looked at her son and smiled. "All right, if you think that's best," she said. "I guess it's time Nathan heard the whole story. Rosie's been bugging me to talk to him anyway."

Daniel repositioned his ball cap. "Do you want me to talk to Nathan?" he asked.

"No, I have a few things to explain to him if he's ever going to trust me around his children."

"Okay, then let me get back to work. I'll let you do the talking."

Pulling the box closer to her once again, Marie said, "Now, how about we take a look in this box? Maybe we can figure out who sent it."

Emma moved to the floor, anxious to help her mother untangle the secrets of her past. Pulling the quilt off the top, Emma laid it on her lap just as the corner with the embroidered lily came into sight.

"Most of the quilters I know always add something special to their quilt to make it theirs," she said, running her fingers over the white flower. "What is so special about this quilt?"

"Someone sent it to your father and me right after we married."

"Do you know who sent it?"

"No. We never did figure it out. I thought at one point your father knew, but when I asked him, he changed the subject."

Emma studied the quilt for a minute. "I think I know who sent it."

"How?"

"Look at this flower. It's a white lily. Maybe Lilian Shetler, who runs Lily's Quilt Shop, had something to do with it."

"Oh my, I think you're right. Nathan has a quilt on his bed just like this but in different colors, and there is the same white lily embroidered in the corner. I shouldn't have been in his room so I couldn't ask him about it. But I bet Rosie will know."

Emma looked up at her mother. "Do you really think Rosie knows more than she's let on?"

"That woman is full of secrets, I'm sure of it. For some reason, she thinks God orchestrated me coming back to Sugarcreek and working for Nathan. She says it's all part of His grander plan. Rosie claims it's as clear as anything, and I'm just not seeing it. Still not sure what she's talking about, but she's always saying things I don't understand."

Emma sat with the quilt on her lap, admiring the beautiful blue and gray fabric, giving a lot of thought to what her mother had said. Folding the blanket and putting it on the floor beside her, she said, "Ya know, maybe Rosie is right. Think about it. Daniel's adopted father moved him to Willow Springs and I was kept safe far away from the English court system. Daniel couldn't find you a place to live and brought you back here, and Nathan gave you a job surrounded by Jake's family. Lastly, Rosie and Lilian are friends. How could all of this come together if not planned out by *Gott*? Even my *mamm* thinks He has something in mind pulling us all together."

169

Feeling puddles form in the corners of her eyes, Marie looked away. "But you don't understand," she said, sighing. "God doesn't care about me."

Pushing the box away from her mother's feet, Emma crawled closer to Marie and sat on her heels. Picking up her mother's hands, she commanded, "Momma, look at me."

The warmth Marie felt from her daughter's touch filled her with hope. Looking into Emma's brown eyes, a reflection of her late husband's, she saw a young woman who clearly was filled with God's love. Memories flashed back as she remembered the faith she once had as well.

Waiting for her mother to focus on her, Emma continued, "You have it all wrong. *Gott* does care, and He's never forgotten or left you. He has always been right beside you, waiting for you to call His name. He never left you; you left Him."

Emma gave her mother a moment to take in what she'd said. "I have no idea what it was like living in prison or even being married to my father, but I believe *Gott* was with you all along. Daniel and I both agree that He protected us for you when you couldn't. But look. He brought us back to you when you needed us the most. I had no idea what it was going to be like getting to know you, but I've had peace about it from day one."

She stopped her flood of words to squeeze her mother's hand.

"Peace like that only comes from *Gott,*" she continued. "You have to believe the only person who's keeping you from *Gott* is you."

The tears Marie fought rolled down her cheeks and dripped onto Emma's hands. Pulling her hand from Emma's, she wiped them off. "I was baptized in the Mennonite church when I was sixteen," she said. "Shortly after that I met your father. He was so against any form of religion after his family shunned him that he asked me to stop covering my head. That's when I stopped going to church. I struggled with that for years. I felt I disappointed God for choosing your father over Him."

Emma shifted in her chair. "I know I'm not very old, and maybe these things would come better from the Bishop or even Nathan, but for some reason, I knew *Gott* was telling me I was supposed to go

170

to you," she said, her tone serious. "I have no ill feelings toward you and have always felt that I was meant to tell you He has not forgotten about you. I've never felt stronger about anything else in my life. I even went against my *datt* in coming here because I felt so strongly about it."

Marie reached over to take her daughter's hand. "And maybe it was you who was supposed to remind me of that. How did I get so lucky to have a daughter who was open enough to tell me like it is?"

Pulling the box over to her one more time, Marie reached in and pulled out the next item in the stack. "It's my mother's Bible." She ran her palm over the black well-worn leather cover and let her fingers open to the spot that was marked with a thick bookmark. Opening the page to Corinthians 11, a chapter she knew well, she stopped to read the words printed on the flowery card stock. "IF YOU SENSE YOUR FAITH IS UNRAVELING, GO BACK TO WHERE YOU DROPPED THE THREAD OF OBEDIENCE."

Taking a moment to re-read the message, Marie handed the bookmark to Emma. "Isn't that fitting? It's like someone put that there just for me to read."

Emma smiled and handed it back to her. "See, how can you not think *Gott* has his hand in all of this?"

"Emma, someone marked this chapter for me to read. This book in the Bible talks about a woman's head covering. This is the chapter I studied over and over again when your father insisted I stop covering my head. No one, not even my own mother, knew the turmoil I was in over this very chapter."

Closing the Bible and reaching in the box for what was next, Marie pulled out a package wrapped in tissue paper. Unfolding it carefully on her lap, she looked up at Emma when the contents came into view. "My prayer veils?"

"Who would have sent these to you?" Emma asked, her voice puzzled. "It had to be someone who had access to your things. Your mother?"

"Maybe, but she died fifteen years ago. Someone would have had to hold on to this stuff all this time and know where I was to get them to me."

Marie picked up the circle of black lace. "I know these are mine because my mother and I made them. She let me pick out the lace, and we handstitched the scallop design around the edges together. I learned how to make tiny even stitches on these veils."

Emma reached in the box and pulled out the next item. Looking over to her mother before unwrapping the bundle in white paper, she asked, "Can I?"

"Go ahead."

Emma gently undid the package, anxious to see what was inside. Inside the paper was a plain, handmade, light-blue dress. She held it up for Marie to see. "Someone made this. I saw some Mennonite women wearing this style in town the other day."

Marie admired the dress. "This is the pattern of dress the women at my mother's church wore. It's much like the dress I wore when I went to church there."

Holding up the dress and sizing it against her mother's shape, Emma said, "It looks like they made it just for you."

Looking in the box one last time, Marie saw everything had been removed except a single pink envelope on the bottom. She reached inside and held it in her hand. Concentrating on the name written in perfect penmanship on the outside, she lifted her head toward Emma. Tears in her eyes, she said, "This is my mother's handwriting."

"How can that be?"

"I'm not sure. I can't read it." Handing it to Emma, she said, "Here, you read it out loud."

Emma took the letter and carefully unstuck the flap. She removed the pink stationery that had been placed inside, so many years ago.

May 28, 2002

Marie,

If you are reading this letter, then I can only hope you've found your way back to Sugarcreek. I know my time here on earth is about to come to an end. For some reason, the good Lord is calling me

172

home and away from you, Daniel and Elizabeth. I'm so sorry I'm not able to take care of Daniel like I promised. I am not sure what will happen to him, but I'm confident God has a plan for his life.

I have so many things to tell you, and since I'm not sure I'll ever get to see you again, I feel the need to leave this letter for you. If you're reading this, then I am sure you already know I've left these things for you to be delivered when the time is right. Please know I'm not proud of how I handled things when you walked away from the church. I was upset that you chose Jake over your God. But, now I understand that it is what you had to do at the time. We all have to grow in our own faith, and the Lord often puts us in situations where we have to rely on Him to see us through. You had to grow and mature in your own way, and nothing I did or said could change any of that. I pushed you away when I should have held you close. For that, I'm sorry.

I've had many conversations with Jake's parents over the last few weeks, and even though they hated to do it, they too had to follow the Ordnung of their Church and turn their backs on Jake and his wild ways. They prayed that he would come back to the church and repent, but once they realized he had changed his name, they knew they had lost him forever. They are good people and just wanted to see their son come back to them and his church. And just so you know, they hold no hard feelings toward you. Walter Troyer explained to them what happened the day Jake died. They know you did what you had to do to save another man's life. It was hard for them to admit he had a drinking problem and they knew he wasn't in his right mind most of the time. Melvin and Lilian have promised to watch over Elizabeth and see to it that Daniel is always cared for. I'm not sure they will have much say in Daniel's life, but I can rest in knowing they will always have a hand in Elizabeth's. She will be safe with the Bylers.

Marie, please know I tried the best I could to raise you, and I didn't always do everything right, but I did turn to God often. He never let me down, and he will never let you down either. Please find your way back to Him and know that I will be waiting with open arms when it is your time to join me in God's special place.

Emma stopped long enough to wipe her nose on her sleeve and look over at her mother, whose tears were flowing freely. She took a deep breath and continued.

I'm sure you've wondered why I didn't leave this house or any of your father's property to you. I wanted to make sure you were always taken care of, so I have signed over everything I own to Melvin Shetler. I have faith he will use it to help pay for any fees you incur or to help you get back on your feet once you've been released.

If you've found your way back to my grandchildren, please tell them that I love them, and my heart is heavy that I didn't live long enough to know them better. Daniel is a sweet boy and has taken care of me the best way a six-year-old could. Please tell Elizabeth how sorry I am I could not keep her close to me, but Lilian promised she would see that she never needed for anything. So many secrets she'll have to come to know. My only hope is the Bylers will raise her to have a forgiving heart and that she'll not hold it against anyone who has kept her birth family from her for so long. God willing, it's all in His control now.

Lastly, I can tell by the few letters we've exchanged that you are mad at God. Marie, it's not too late. Go back to where you lost all hope and pick back up where you left off. God is waiting for you to call on Him. He wants to hear your voice.

Until we see each other again,
All my love,
Momma

Putting the letter on the stand between them, Emma knelt in front of her mother and laid her head on her lap. Marie took the back of her hand and wiped the tears from the side of her daughter's cheek. Her own tears were falling on the top of Emma's starched white *kapp*.

Chapter 19 - Meet me on the Porch

Marie no sooner took the ham and potato casserole out of the oven when Nathan and Daniel walked in the side door. Emma was finishing setting the table when Daniel spoke up.

"No need to set the other places tonight; the guys have plans. It's just the six of us."

Picking up the extra plates, Emma returned them to the cupboard without saying a word. There was a quietness in the room as Marie and Emma moved around the table, making sure everything was ready for supper.

Standing at the sink waiting to wash his hands, Daniel eyed Nathan and furrowed his eyebrows in a questioning manner. Nathan shrugged his shoulders and slightly shook his head, feeling the tension in the room as well.

Trying to lighten the mood, Daniel looked over his shoulder toward Rachel. "How about we try and get Emma back on her bike after supper?"

"Can we, Emma?"

"Maybe," Emma said, taking her seat across from Daniel. "I have a headache right now, but I'm hoping once I eat, it will go away. Let's see how I feel in a little bit. Why don't you tell your *datt* about picking apples today?"

As soon as Nathan finished the prayer, Rachel started telling him all about their day at Anna Mae's.

"Emma and I made apple crisp. Can you smell it?"

Nathan took a deep breath and rubbed his stomach. "I sure can, and it smells wonderful. I'll make sure I save room."

Handing his plate to Marie as she filled everyone's plate from the hot dish in the center of the table, he asked, "Did *Mamm* eat yet?"

"I took her a plate right before you came in. I think she misses being at the table with us, but it's just so hard for her to get around. I was going to ask you if you thought we could get her a wheelchair. I know she'll fight us on it, but she'd feel so much better if she didn't have to stay in her room all day. Her mind is sharp, and she still wants to be around everyone. Emma and I have such a hard time getting her from one place to the next when you're not in the house."

Nathan took his plate back from Marie. "That's a great idea," he said. "I'm not sure why I didn't think of that. I'll talk to her about it later."

Both Marie and Emma did more pushing their food around their plates than eating it. It took Daniel only a few minutes of watching them both before he spoke up.

"What is with the two of you?"

Rachel didn't wait for them to answer before she piped in. "They were sad today."

Daniel looked at Emma and then to his mother. "Did something happen we should know about?"

Rachel reached for her cup. "They cried today," she added. "Like I did when *Mamm* went to live with Jesus."

Daniel put down his fork. Nathan did the same.

Looking at Rachel, Nathan said, "How about you let them tell us what happened."

In the middle of buttering Amos a slice of bread, Marie looked toward Rachel. Quietly, she spoke. "Emma and I were sad today."

Taking a few seconds to gather her thoughts, she continued. "Sometimes, when things happen that upset you, it takes a few hours to shake the blue mood it puts you in. I'm sorry you had to see us cry. But not all tears are sad. Sometimes you cry because you're happy. We had both happy and sad tears today. Right, Emma?"

Wanting to help Marie make Rachel feel better about seeing them cry, Emma agreed. "That's exactly right, and you know what? I feel better just talking about it. I think we're done being sad now. Let's eat so you and Daniel can get back to teaching me to ride."

Looking toward Daniel, she whispered, "I'll tell you later."

176

Marie felt Nathan looking at her before she looked up to meet his gaze. Mouthing "later" in the same hushed tone, she picked up her fork and turned her attention to Amos.

~~

Needing a few minutes alone before she got up enough nerve to talk to Nathan, Marie pushed Emma outside and volunteered to clean the kitchen by herself. Standing at the sink watching Daniel carry Amos closer to the driveway to cheer Emma on, she caught herself whispering a small prayer thanking God for bringing her children back into her life. Then she shook her head in disbelief. *Where did that come from? Maybe it was everything in the box, or perhaps it was her mother's letter that stirred something inside her. Could it be that easy? Could she pick up her faith right where she dropped it?*

Not hearing Nathan come in the room, she jumped when she turned around to see him standing in the doorway between the kitchen and the sitting room.

"Did you hear me? *Mamm* thought a wheelchair would be a good idea."

"Oh, good. I think it will help her from feeling so isolated. The rooms are plenty big enough around here that she can get around from room to room easily."

She held up the pot of coffee she had just made. "I was going to have a cup; would you like some? We could sit on the porch and watch the kids if you'd like."

"Sure. Then maybe you can tell me what went on today."

"I will."

At the edge of the porch steps, Nathan smiled watching Emma pedal her first solo ride. Rachel and Amos clapped and hollered as she finally mastered balancing on two wheels. It was good to see them have fun. He couldn't help laughing along with them.

Hearing the screen door shut behind him, he turned and reached for the cup Marie handed him.

177

"Well, look at that," she said, watching her daughter wheeling down the driveway. "I'd say Emma's figured it out. It's a shame it took her sixteen years to learn how to ride, but I'm glad Daniel was the one who taught her."

Taking a sip from his cup, Nathan smiled. *Perfect, again. Almost better than Suzy's. Emma must have taught her how to use the percolator.*

He nodded to the chairs under the front window. "Shall we?"

Letting the stillness of the evening air fill the emptiness between them, Nathan gave Marie plenty of time to gather her thoughts. Gripping her coffee mug with both hands, she rested its bottom on her lap and began. "I have a few things I'd like to talk to you about."

Not entirely sure where the conversation was going, Nathan replied in a stern but calming tone. "I'm all ears."

Marie took a deep breath. "I think I know why the Bishop is pushing me to go to church and why he's forced your hand in hiring me. But before I tell you, I want you to know you can let me go at any time. I know being here wasn't your idea, and I don't want you to feel like you have to keep me on with some obligation to Daniel or the Bishop."

She didn't expect him to say anything, but the way he looked straight ahead and didn't respond made her uncomfortable. She chose to continue.

"I need to tell you about my life with Jake. Maybe then you'll feel better about me taking care of your children. I met Jake while waiting tables. He used to come in with a group of his friends a couple times a week and always sat in my section. At first, I thought he was English and only found out later he was on his *Rumshpringa*. He had gotten himself mixed up with a bunch of troublemakers. He swept me off my feet, and before I knew it, he had been disowned by his family, and I found myself pregnant."

Nathan continued to look straight ahead. "So he was Amish?"

"Yes, and I was raised in a liberal Mennonite church."

He finally turned his head in her direction. "Here in Sugarcreek?"

"Yes. My father died when I was little, and my mother tried her best to give me a Christian upbringing. I had already been baptized

178

when I met Jake, and getting pregnant was hard on her. I think he married me out of duty more than anything else. He had a lot of his own issues, and I think we weren't old enough or mature enough to handle marriage. I could never get him to stop hanging out with his group of friends, and his drinking got awful. The beer wasn't so bad, but when he mixed it with the hard stuff, there was no stopping his rages."

Crossing her legs and setting the cup on the table between them, Marie let Nathan absorb what she had shared so far.

"There are parts of my life I've blocked out, but I remember feeling like I was in survival mode," she continued, determined to finish. "My instinct was to keep Daniel out of his way and safe. I dropped him off at my mother's a good bit, which only angered him more. As I look back on it, I think he felt he couldn't control anything in his life but me. And he did that with a heavy hand."

Dredging up old memories made Marie's palms sweat, but she knew she needed to explain everything if Nathan was going to trust her. Part of her wanted to run away and not dig into things she'd just soon forget. But the other part of her felt safe in knowing he deserved to hear it all.

"Only a few people know what happened the day Jake died. Me, Anna Mae Troyer's late husband Walter, and Emma's father, Jacob. Oh, and Bishop Shetler."

"The Bishop? How does he work into all of this?"

"You'll see. Let me finish."

For the next twenty minutes, Marie explained how she'd saved Jacob and how she took all the blame in Jake's death. Letting him know how she refused to tell the police about Walter, for fear they would find out about Emma. If she would have let Walter back up her story, she probably wouldn't have had to spend any time behind bars, but she couldn't chance anyone finding out that she'd given Emma to Walter. She even went into great detail on how she believed the Bishop had protected Emma and kept the police from interviewing Jacob.

Nathan leaned forward and rested his elbows on his knees. "But I still don't understand the Bishop's involvement in all of this. What did he have to gain in sending Emma to Willow Springs?"

179

"Because Emma was his granddaughter. Jake was Bishop Shetler's oldest son."

"But I thought you said you didn't know who Jake's family was."

"I didn't, and Jake only took me to see his mother once, and she wasn't too welcoming. I'd only figured that out today when Emma and I read my mother's letter."

Taking a second to think about what she had said, Nathan cocked his head toward Marie. "Jake Shetler? I went to school with him. I never knew what happened to him. I heard he left to go live with the English. How did I not hear he died?"

"Because he changed his name to Cooper. Even if you did read about it, you'd never have put two and two together. As I see it, Bishop Shetler did everything in his power to brush it under the rug."

Sitting back up, Nathan ran his hand through his hair. "*Mamm* is good friends with Lilian. I'm surprised she's never said anything."

"Oh, believe me, your *mamm* knows more than she's let on. I'm pretty sure she knows my whole story, including who Jake was. She's been pushing me to tell you everything for days now."

"Now this surely puts a whole new twist on things," Nathan said. "What are you going to do now?"

Turning his attention to the yard, Nathan watched Daniel lift Amos off the ground and onto his shoulders. "We're taking a walk to the creek," Daniel hollered. "We'll be back shortly."

Nathan raised his hand to acknowledge he'd heard, giving Marie plenty of time to respond to his question.

"Well, that all depends on a few things," she replied, picking up her cup and pushing her foot to set her chair in motion. "First, I'd like to talk to Jake's parents. I'm sure they can answer a few questions I have. According to my mother's letter, she signed over her estate to Melvin. If that's the case there may be some money left I can use to get on my feet. That way, you wouldn't feel like you have to keep me on."

Not sure how he felt about her last comment, Nathan stayed quiet.

180

"Next, I guess it depends on Emma and Daniel. I can tell Emma is homesick, and I don't want her to think she has to take care of me. She has a life back in Willow Springs, and she needs to get back to it. I'm not sure about Daniel. He's mentioned he feels more at home here."

A warm breeze blew past her nose and stirred the windchime at the end of the porch. Turning her head toward the sound, she waited for the metal tubes to stop singing. "That's about as much thought as I've given it, other than Daniel suggesting I ask you to talk to the Bishop for me. I hate to put you in the middle, and I'll understand if you don't want to."

Nathan rose and walked to the edge of the porch. Hooking his thumbs in his suspenders, he said, "I think the Bishop has an agenda all of his own. Thinking back to our conversations over the last couple weeks, he's put me more in the middle than you even realize."

"What do you mean?"

Without answering, Nathan walked down the steps. "I'll be leaving around eight in the morning. We'll talk to him together after the worship service."

Watching his long strides across the yard, Marie realized she was quickly learning that when Nathan Bouteright was bothered by something, he found solitude in the stables.

~~

Waking long before the alarm clock chimed six, Marie sat on the side of the bed, waiting for the first morning light to filter into the room she shared with Emma. Looking at the tissue-wrapped package on the chair, she struggled with the pull it had on her. As a young woman, she wouldn't dream of walking into church or even praying without her head covered. And now, after so many years of going against every ounce of doctrine she'd been taught, did she think a simple circle of black lace would change her heart? Remembering the bookmark she'd found in her mother's Bible, she couldn't help but feel the day Jake made her stop wearing her head covering was the day she started to lose her faith. Was that the spot where she'd dropped her thread of obedience?

Emma's voice broke her trance.

"Are you all right?"

"I guess I'm a little nervous about today," she replied. "Working for Nathan is one thing, but going to an Amish service – I'm not so sure about that."

"It won't be as bad as you think. The Ministers are used to Nathan bringing English to the service. And besides, if you want to talk to the Bishop you'll need to go."

"Oh, I'm going. I'm just not very comfortable about it."

Emma stood to make her bed. Reaching for her clothes, she said, "How about I go get dressed and head over to start breakfast? I'll make sure Rachel and Amos are up, and I'll warm up the egg and sausage casserole. You take your time and come over when you're ready."

"That would be great," Marie said, not moving from the side of the bed. "Thank you."

Waiting until Emma left the room before she reached for the bundle, Marie slowly unwrapped it and worked through the emotions it stirred. Holding the lacy fabric in her hands, she looked toward the blue dress that lay neatly over the back of the chair. *What I wear isn't going to make one bit of difference in how people treat me, and it surely isn't going to make me feel any closer to God.* Laying the tissue paper on her bed, she walked to the peg by the door and retrieved her jean skirt. She looked at the skirt and back to the plain dress. *Mom, how could you think a simple dress and head covering would help me find myself again? You really can't expect me to walk back into a life I left so long ago. Can you?*

No matter how hard she tried to deny it, the conviction she felt now was as strong as the day she chose to bear all the burden of Jake's death. It was something she knew she had to do.

Twisting her hair in a bun and covering it with one of Emma's hair nets, Marie pinned the covering to the back of her head as quickly as if she'd been doing it all her life. Slipping the plain dress over her head, she walked to the window just as the sun's pink and yellow rays started to peek above the horizon. The sunflowers lining the garden outside her bedroom window had yet to lift their heads to the sun. They shone like gold rays against the pale blue sky that was just starting to light the day. Closing her tear-filled eyes, she heard herself whisper. "Dear Lord, I don't understand the path you have for me. Please forgive me for being gone from you for so long. Help me see your face and hear your voice. In Jesus' name, Amen."

Opening her eyes to see one of Nathan's horses run through the pasture, Marie felt an instant connection to the animal. It gracefully moved around the fenced-in area, running in circles and free to move as it wished as long as it stayed within the confines of its protected barrier. Much like how she felt the minute she pinned on her veil. Free from her past and protected by God's grace. Leaning her forehead against the cool glass, she closed her eyes. "Thy kingdom come; thy will be done on earth as it is in heaven," she whispered.

The room suddenly felt warm even though the goosebumps on her arms crawled clear up to the back of her neck. She refused to open her eyes, afraid the peace she felt would dissolve. Letting the sun filter through the window and onto her face, she thought to herself, *Thank you, Momma, you always knew exactly what I needed even before I knew myself.*

Walking across the yard feeling the warm morning sun on the back of her neck, Marie felt her anxiety about the day ease away. Closer to the porch she noticed Nathan standing directly behind the screened door. His expression confused her. Stopping and waiting for him to push the door open or step aside, she couldn't break away from his gaze, so steadily he kept his eyes locked to hers. Silently he pushed the door open and held it for her to enter. Marie walked through, his closeness sending shivers down her arms. Finally she dropped her eyes, thinking, *What on earth is that all about?*

Chapter 20 - The Bishop

After dropping Emma, Marie, and the *kinner* off at the front of the house where worship was being held, Nathan pulled the buggy to the side of the barn. Taking a few minutes before he unhooked his horse and led it to the line strung between two fence posts in the field, he waited inside. Letting the thoughts he'd pushed away for the last hour surface to the front of his mind, he played over in his head the sight of Marie walking across the yard. The sun, breaking the horizon behind her, surrounded her with a warm glow. There was no denying it stirred something deep inside as he watched her walk toward him. Confused by his own reaction, he shook his head and jumped down from the buggy. Busying himself tending to his horse, he glanced over at the group of men gathering around the barn. He was in no hurry to join them.

Turning his attention to the house where the women lined up by the back door waiting to file inside, he looked for Marie. Her light blue dress stood out from the dark colors and white *kapps* of the women in his *g'may*. He could sense she felt uncomfortable from the way she was trying to stand firmly behind Emma and Rachel. Watching her balance Amos on her hip, he wished he would have kept the boy with him.

Handing the rope he used to tether his horse to one of the boys helping with the buggies, Nathan walked to where the women stood. Reaching to take Amos from Marie, he said, "I'll keep him with me this morning. He's too heavy for you to be carrying."

Without waiting for her to object, he turned and walked back to the barn. For some reason, her presence was unnerving him this morning. He needed to keep his distance.

"Nathan, wait." Closing the gap between them, Marie walked away from the line to talk to him in private. "Will you talk to the Bishop with me this morning?

Stopping in his tracks as she got closer, he turned and couldn't help but be eye-to-eye with her. There was a softness in her voice he hadn't heard before. For weeks he saw her as hard and unreachable. An unlikely choice for a caretaker for his family. An inconvenience and nothing else. But something changed in him last night listening to her share her life story. The harsh tone that had already started to form on his lips turned to compassion as he looked at her.

"I'll talk to him after the fellowship meal."

Marie looked over his shoulder to the group of men clearly looking their way. "I hope my being here doesn't cause you too much grief," she said.

Turning his head in the direction of the barn, Nathan smiled. "Oh, believe me, it's not your presence they're gawking at."

"What do you mean?"

Leaning in a little closer, he whispered, "I'll tell you later."

Watching him walk away, she couldn't help but smile at his unusual, playful tone.

Finding her way back to where Emma and Rachel stood, Marie stopped when she heard her name. Rotating in the direction of the voice behind her, she was surprised to see Lilian Shetler standing in the side yard, motioning for her to come closer. Not sure she was ready to have a conversation with Jake's mother, she hesitated. Taking in a deep breath and squaring her shoulders, she headed her way.

The woman's demeanor was completely different from the day before. The unaccepting attitude at the bulk foods store had changed to a warm welcome.

"Marie, it's so good to see you joining us this morning."

"Thank you," was all Marie could get out. Her mother's letter played over in her head as she tried to decide if she should let on she knew who Lilian was. Before she got a chance to respond, Lilian looked around to make sure no one was close and continued.

185

"I'm sure you have questions for me, and in due time I will answer them all. But this morning, I have something for you."

Reaching in her pocket, she pulled out a simple white handkerchief. Taking Marie's hand in her own, she laid the starched white piece of linen in her hand. The familiar monogrammed letters of her mother's initials brought another emotion to the surface.

"Where did you get this?" Lillian heard the sharpness in her voice.

"Your mother wanted me to give it to you when the time was right."

Marie rubbed her fingers over the navy blue embroidered initials. "I made this for her," she said.

"I know. She wanted you to have it back. I promised her I would see that it was returned to you."

Looking down at the woman who favored both Emma and Jake, she felt an instant bond to her. "It was you who sent the box, right?"

"Yes, I did. I spent a lot of time with your mother before she died and we became fast friends. She picked the fabric for that dress, and we made it together before she passed."

Lilian reached over to lay her hand on Marie's arm. "I'm sorry for all you've been through. I hope someday you will forgive me for the part I've played in all of it."

Looking back toward the line of women, Lilian said, "We can talk later." Then she leaned in close, her voice becoming soft. "You're among friends now — and family when you're ready."

Not sure what to make of their short conversation, Marie stood grounded, holding tightly to her mother's hankie. Watching as the group of men started to make their way across the yard and into the house, she noticed Nathan hand Amos off and head towards her.

"What did Lilian want?"

Marie showed him what was in her hand. "She wanted to give me this."

"A hankie?"

"Not just a hankie, but my mother's handkerchief."

"How on earth did she get that?"

"By what she tells me, she and my mother were friends." Looking down at her dress, she said, "Lilian helped my mother make

186

this and promised her before she died she'd see to it I got it when the time was right. I guess she felt this morning was the right time. As for the hankie, I made it for her."

"Then Lilian sent you the box and your mother's letter?"

"Yes."

Nodding in the direction of Daniel, Nathan watched his slouched form move to the back of the line of men waiting to go inside. "Do you have any idea what his problem is this morning?" Nathan asked. "It's not like him to be so quiet."

"I hate to admit it, but I've been so wrapped up in my own emotions this morning I didn't notice. I saw him talking to Emma, so maybe she knows. I'll ask her."

"We'd better get inside." Nathan headed to the house.

Walking beside him until they got closer, Nathan went up the front steps as Marie headed for the side door and entered through the kitchen. Finding an open seat at the back of the room, she quietly sank on the bench and listened as the song leader sang the first few words of the opening song. In another room, a clock rang nine chimes as the slow acapella song gave the room a divine ambiance. Looking around for Emma and Daniel, she was surprised to see Daniel sing the foreign words as easily as Emma. Remembering him say he'd spent a good part of his teenage years at Nathan's, she smiled as she watched how he enjoyed the song.

Not understanding everything that was being preached she took time adjusting to her new surroundings. The Bishop was the last to speak, and he made a point to repeat many of his passages in English for her to understand. For most of his sermon she felt as if he had meant it just for her. The list of questions she had organized in her head was getting longer as she tried not to forget any of them. She was getting anxious to talk to the Bishop and his wife and hoped Nathan would get a chance to speak with them before they left.

After the last song she followed Emma to the kitchen, only stopping when Rachel pulled on her sleeve. "Marie, can I go out and play before lunch?"

Stopping and looking at Emma to be sure it was allowed before she gave the girl her approval, she waved her on out the door.

Marie grabbed Emma's arm before they got to the kitchen. "I'm not sure I'm ready to be in the thick of things. Do you mind if I step outside for a few minutes?"

"No problem. I'm sure Nathan would like to have a break from Amos."

Stepping out on the porch and scanning the yard, she headed in Nathan's direction once she found him in the crowd. Standing near the corner of the barn, he had set Amos on a tree stump as he stood with one leg propped on a log.

Amos eagerly waved in her direction. "Marie, here we are," he hollered.

Waving back, she headed their way. "I thought I'd give your *datt* a break. How about you hang out with me for a few minutes?"

Nathan looked at the Bishop and back to Marie. "Perfect timing. Let me go see if I can get him to stop over on his way home. It's time we all figure out his role in all of this."

Scooting Amos over enough to sit beside him, Marie watched as Nathan walked toward the gray-bearded man.

~~

Extending his hand to him as he approached, Nathan weighed his words before he began. "I'd like to talk to you about a few things if you have a minute."

"I do until they tell us lunch is ready." Patting his belly, the Bishop continued, "I wouldn't want to be the last to the table."

He looked in Marie's direction. "I assume you want to know if I asked around to see if there were any older available women who would agree to a marriage of convenience."

Nathan also glanced in Marie's direction. "Actually, that wasn't on my mind at this very moment."

Taking longer than usual to take his eyes off her, he turned to face the Bishop. "She filled me in about a lot of things yesterday, and I'm pretty sure you and Lilian can help her get to the bottom of a few of them."

Ignoring his comment, the Bishop went back to his original question. "So, you've changed your mind about finding a *fraa* to take care of your *kinner?"*

In a frustrated tone, Nathan responded, "I'm not worried about that right now; I'm more concerned with Marie getting the answers she deserves. For the past sixteen years, she's been kept in the dark about so many things. Don't you think you owe her, Emma and Daniel an explanation?"

The Bishop pulled on his beard, taking his time to answer. "Maybe so," he finally said. "But not here. We'll stop on our way home."

~~

Putting Amos down for a nap and instructing Rachel to play in her room, Marie listened as Nathan answered the door and led Melvin and Lilian into the house. She had left Emma and Daniel in the kitchen and was sure they had all sat around the table waiting for her to come back downstairs. Unsure she wanted to dredge Jake back up, she knew the conversation would center around her late husband's life. Facing his parents in such an open manner made her anxious, but she knew for the sake of her children it was something she must do.

Standing on the top step, straining to hear the conversation that had already started, she quietly began walking down the steps, taking each one as slowly as she could. For some reason, she had an uneasy feeling she couldn't shake.

Emma had already made a pot of coffee and placed a plate of cookies in the center of the table as they waited for her to take a seat. It was the Bishop who spoke first. He looked at Marie when he did.

"By now you know Jake was our oldest son. We mourned his loss long before he died when he made his choice to leave the Church. He had already been baptized, so we had to put him in the *bann*. It was our only hope that he would make it back to us someday. We knew his drinking had gotten out of hand, but he left

189

us no choice; our hands were tied, and besides I had just been appointed Bishop."

Marie twisted a paper napkin in her hands and looked to Lilian. "Do you remember Jake bringing me to meet you? He was so excited we were pregnant; he couldn't wait to tell you. You wouldn't even talk to him. He was crushed by your response."

Lilian looked toward her husband before she answered. "You have to understand, I was forbidden to talk to him. He put me in a difficult situation, and one I kept from my husband for all of these years. No matter how excited I was for the both of you, I couldn't show it."

Marie put her hands on her lap. "After I had Daniel, Jake's drinking got much worse. There was no reasoning with him. Some days were better than others."

Stopping to make sure what she wanted to share with them wouldn't come across in the wrong way, she continued slowly. "You have to know he felt he could never measure up to you, and there was nothing he could do to make you proud. All he ever wanted was your approval. He made a table for our apartment and wished he could show it to you."

"I saw the table, and he did a fine job on it," the Bishop said, his voice cracking slightly. "I knew his skills as a furniture maker were as good or better than mine or any of his brothers."

Curious, Marie asked, "How did you see the table?"

"I cleaned out your apartment. That table and all of your belongings are stored in a spare bedroom in our home. They are yours whenever you want or need them."

Emma interrupted. "So is that how my *datt* got my birth certificate and the picture of Daniel and me?"

"It is."

Emma had her own questions and waited for her grandfather to stop before asking the one that had consumed her for the last twenty-four hours.

"If you knew about me, why did you send me away?"

He dropped his head. When he looked back up, his eyes had misted over. "The one thing I've struggled with my whole life. Pride."

This time it was Daniel who spoke up. Pushing his chair back and standing up, he said in a louder than normal voice. "Pride! You knew your son had two children who had just lost their mother and father and you let pride stand in the way. I spent years being bounced around in foster homes when I had family all along. I was your grandson, and you couldn't see past your pride to take me in? Do you have any idea what I went through?"

Marie looked sternly at her son. "Daniel, please calm down and let him explain."

"Calm down! I've been nothing but calm for the past twenty-one years. I stayed calm as I watched my father mistreat you, I stayed calm when I watched my grandmother die. I stayed calm as I watched every little boy get adopted but me. I even stayed calm when I found out you signed your parental rights away. Now you want me to stay calm when I find out I had family all along who could have taken me in. And all because he was too embarrassed to admit one of his children left his precious church."

Standing over the sink with his back to everyone, Daniel kept going. "You knew who I was all along, didn't you? You treated me different than the other stable hands."

Melvin looked in his direction. "Daniel, I may not have taken you in, but I've always played a part in your life. I always knew where you were. We used part of your grandmother's estate to give the Millers the money needed to adopt you. They had no idea where the money came from, but we made sure they had it."

Daniel picked up his ball cap from the table and headed to the door. "I've heard enough." His voice was sharp.

The screen door rattled the clock on the wall. Nathan looked to Marie. "Let him go."

Marie eyed Melvin. "So all these years when I had no idea where Elizabeth was, you knew all along? You have no idea how I agonized about not knowing what happened to her."

Taking in a long breath and blowing it out slowly, he weighed his words carefully. "Just like Daniel, I always knew how she was. Jacob made sure of that. Whether you believe it or not, I kept a close eye on both of my grandchildren. I knew when the time was right, I would let them both know who their family was. I hadn't planned on Elizabeth becoming Emma Byler. It just happened. When I sent her home with Jacob and Stella it was just until I could figure out what to do next. Stella had just lost her *boppli,* and it only made sense to me that *Gott* put her in my path for a reason."

"And the letters?"

"I asked Jacob to hold off on explaining things to her until you got released. There was no sense in upsetting her life until she was old enough to understand the choices we made."

Emma took a tissue from her pocket and wiped her nose. "So, my parents knew I had family here?"

"Only your *datt* and his Bishop. I'm pretty sure your *mamm* has no idea."

"You played *Gott,*" Emma whispered, not realizing she'd said it out loud.

"Elizabeth," Lilian reprimanded, startled.

"It's Emma," she interrupted in a correcting tone. "Remember the name given to my *mamm's* dead *boppli.*"

Nathan stood. "I think we've had just about enough for one day. It's going to take time for us to make sense of all of this. There is nothing we can do to change the past. Whether we understand your reasoning or not, this is the path *Gott* has us on, and we need to be obedient enough to follow it through."

He turned his attention to the Bishop. "Can I talk to you outside for a few minutes?"

Not answering but standing to follow Nathan through the front room, the men went outside.

Nathan was the first to speak. "Thank you for stopping by this afternoon. I'm sure once Daniel has had a chance to absorb it all, he'll come around. And Emma, she's pretty easygoing. After she gets over the shock of her *datt* knowing more than he let on, she'll come around."

Melvin twirled his hat by the rim. "People think just because I'm Bishop, I have all the answers. I don't. I make mistakes just like everyone else. Did I handle things perfectly? Probably not, but I always did what I thought *Gott* was telling me to do. You have to believe me when I say I thought I was doing what was right for all of them. Looking back on it, maybe I didn't honor my son by raising his *kinner.*"

He let out a long sigh and gazed out over the farm. "What's done is done," he said heavily. "I can't change any of that."

Letting silence fill the air between them, Nathan leaned on the porch railing and crossed his arms over his chest. "I have to ask what motive you had for sending Sarah home and forcing me to hire Marie. What purpose do I have in your plan?"

The Bishop looked toward the stables, assessing his words carefully. Finally, he spoke. "If Marie was going to be accepted in this community, she had to be here with you. You are well respected, and everyone already knows you hire English. They wouldn't think it odd or give me grief about her taking care of your family. It was the only way I could see it work."

Sitting down in the chair opposite Nathan, he rested his elbows on his knees. "I owe it to my son to see that his family is taken care of," he continued. "I was too hard on the boy and probably pushed him away from his faith. I knew he had a drinking problem long before Marie came into the picture. I should have gotten him help, but I was too ashamed. I didn't realize how bad it had gotten until Marie's mother reached out to us. By then, it was too late."

Taking a few minutes to gather his thoughts, the Bishop stood and walked to the edge of the porch. "I haven't let Marie know she has quite a nest egg from her mother. There's no reason she can't get a place of her own. I can even go talk to the manager at the Sugar Valley Restaurant. The only reason he didn't hire her back was because I asked him not to."

Nathan shook his head in disbelief. "I know you thought you were helping, but how I see it, you've been trying to control the outcome of all of their lives for way too long," he said. "It's time you let them follow their own path, not the path you've chosen for them."

The Bishop put his black hat on his head. Pulling the rim even, he said, "I suppose you're right. Well, I think I've overstayed my welcome for one day. Do you mind telling Lilian we're leaving?"

Nathan walked to the edge of the porch and stood alongside the slightly slumping shoulders of his elder. "My door is always open," he said. "You'll never overstay your welcome in my home. Give your grandchildren some time to digest everything, and they will come around. Both of them are good *kinner*. As for Marie, let me handle her."

Raising an eyebrow, Melvin looked in Nathan's direction. "Does that mean you don't want me to help you find a suitable *fraa?*"

"All I'm saying is I'm letting *Gott* find her for me. I have a feeling he put a suitable helpmate right under my nose. My only problem is helping her see it."

Epilogue

After making sure Rachel and Amos were tucked in and that Rosie didn't need anything, Marie poured herself and Nathan a cup of coffee and headed to the porch. Pushing the screen door open with her foot, she stood beside Nathan's chair and handed him his cup. She sat in the chair beside him, holding her cup with both hands close to her mouth. She blew on the hot liquid, then asked, "Have you seen Daniel?"

"I saw him in the stables when I went for my evening rounds. He was brushing Sir Philip. I wouldn't worry about him; he's not prone to sulking for too long. He'll come around."

"I'm a little worried about Emma," Marie said. "She went to bed pretty early. I think she needs to go home to Stella. I might be her mother, but she needs her *mamm,* and I'm okay with that. I'm glad she came, and we got to know each other, but her home is in Willow Springs. I'm going to tell her that tomorrow. I think she feels she needs to stay here and take care of me."

Nathan took a sip of his coffee. "Melvin told me you can afford to find a place of your own if you want. Your mother left you enough; you don't have to stay working here if you'd rather not."

Marie held her breath, taking in the news. Half-afraid of his answer, she asked, "Is that what you want?"

Trying not to scare her away with his response, Nathan turned to look at her. "What I want is for you to wear that color of blue every day. I want you to add just the right amount of milk and sugar to my coffee and sit right beside me as I enjoy it."

Trying to hold back a smile, Marie said, "That's a pretty big order since I only have one dress in this color."

"Well, I can fix that," Nathan said, a slow smile spreading across his face. "I know my way to the fabric store."

"I bet you do, but what you don't realize is I don't know how to make dresses."

"But you see, I know my *mamm* does, and she'd be more than willing to walk you through it."

Setting his cup on the table between them, Nathan reached over and did the same with Marie's. Standing and pulling her up beside him, he wrapped an arm around her waist.

"I know we were forced on one another, but I believe *Gott* had a purpose in mind," he said, eyes focused on the barn where he found refuge. "I'm too young to go through life without a strong woman by my side. And you're too pretty not to have a man tell you so."

Butterflies were doing somersaults in Marie's stomach as she felt herself relax by his touch. The need to flee was replaced by the desire to lean in closer to him. "Are you sure?"

"I've never been more sure about anything. For the past year, I've been begging *Gott* to show me the reason why he took my Suzy from me. Why he left my *kinner* without a *mamm*. I didn't think anyone could love and care for my *kinner* as good as Suzy could. For a short time, I thought that somebody was Sarah, but she wasn't in love with me; I could tell she loved Matthew."

Taking both of her hands in his, Nathan turned Marie around to face him. "And then lo and behold, you came along. Amos fell for you instantly, and I had to stop and take a good look at what he saw in you. When I stood back and started to look at you through his eyes, I saw what he saw. A warm and gentle person who just wanted to be loved. You have to realize it's a man's job to want to take care of those around them. And it doesn't matter if you're four or forty. It's what we're taught to do from an early age."

Marie knew she needed to be honest. "You do realize I have a lot of baggage to work through?"

"I do, and we can work through it together. I'm not sure what the future holds for us, only *Gott* knows that. But I would like to hope you're going to be a big part of it. Please tell me you'll stay. Rachel and Amos need you; even my *Mamm* needs you. She's told me more than once she'd be upset with me if I didn't figure out a way to get you to stay."

Releasing one of her hands, he put his finger under her chin and tipped her head to look in her eyes. Leaning in close enough to brush his lips against hers, he whispered, "Stay."

Whispering back, she said, "I'd like that."

Locked in their embrace, Marie pulled away when she saw Daniel come up the porch steps looking as if he had something important to say.

"Where's Emma?" he asked.

"She went to bed a little bit ago. Is something wrong?"

"When I went up to the loft, I saw Emma's phone had a missed call and message. When I checked the number, it was from Byler's Furniture. I debated on listening to it, but I went ahead and did. Her father said it's vital she come home right away. Do you think I should wake her?"

Marie hesitated. "It's been a long day," she answered. "How about you let her sleep and plan on taking her home in the morning?"

Secrets of Willow Springs - Book 3

December 31, 2017 – Willow Springs, PA

Standing behind Emma trying to protect her from the ice pellets that were stinging the back of his neck, Daniel waited for his sister to tell him she was ready to leave. Everyone who had come to pay their last respects had already added a shovel of dirt to the top of her mother's grave and headed back to their waiting buggies. The sounds of buggy wheels on the frozen ground disappeared, replaced by an unnerving quiet. Emma didn't make a sound as she stood frozen to the spot she had claimed as her own for the past hour. Ignoring the pleas from her *datt* to go back to the *haus* with him, Daniel assured him he would take her home.

Glancing behind him, he noticed the last of the buggies had pulled away from the Amish Cemetery, his truck being the last to leave. Reaching in his pocket for the key, he pressed the remote starter before trying to convince Emma it was time to go. Resting his hands on either side of her shoulders and rubbing her black wool coat to generate heat, he rested his chin on top of her thick brown bonnet.

"The temperature is dropping. Will you please let me take you home now?"

A sob lodged in Emma's throat. It took Daniel a few seconds to understand what she was trying to say. "I don't want to leave her," she said, her voice labored.

Daniel pulled her closer. "I know, but she wouldn't want you standing out here in the cold either."

"I can't believe she's gone. I know this was *Gott's* will, but how am I ever going to live without her?"

Turning her around to wrap his arm around her and guide her to the warmth of his truck, Daniel said, "For a while, I'm sure it's going to be hard."

No sooner had they made it to his truck when a van pulled up beside them. Barely waiting for the white vehicle to come to a complete stop, the side door slid open, and Nathan and Marie got out.

"Mom, Nathan, you came. How did you get permission to leave Ohio?" Daniel asked.

Nathan reached out to shake Daniel's hand. "It took some doing, but we finally got her probation officer to sign the release allowing her to travel to Pennsylvania. We would have been here sooner, but Interstate 80 was a sheet of ice. Our driver couldn't go any faster than forty miles an hour."

It didn't take Emma any time at all to find her way to Marie's open arms.

'Oh, Momma, it happened so fast. The doctors felt certain the chemo would help, but the cancer had already spread to her bones."

Marie wrapped both arms around the girl and pulled her close. "I'm sorry I couldn't get here faster."

"Maybe you'll have better luck getting her out of the cold," Daniel said, blowing warm breath into his cupped hands. "I'm having a hard time getting her to leave."

Breaking the embrace long enough to look in her daughter's eyes, Marie said, "Emma, it's freezing out here. You're not going to do anyone any good if you end up sick. Please, let's get in the van where it's warm."

Nodding her head in agreement, Emma let her mother guide her to the open door.

Daniel pointed to his truck. "Have your driver follow me," he instructed.

Stepping in the van and making her way to the bench seat in the back, Emma took comfort in the warm vehicle. Marie took a seat in the second row and moved over so Nathan could sit beside her. The driver pulled up behind Daniel. It didn't take but a few minutes to catch up to the procession of yellow-topped buggies making their way back to the Byler farm. The stillness in the van was magnified by the slow journey through the back roads of Willow Springs. An overwhelming sadness filled Emma at the thought of returning to the comforts of her *mamm's* kitchen without her in it.

The announcer on the radio reminded her that it was the last day of two thousand and seventeen. A year that would be etched in her memory for the rest of her life. Leaning the side of her head on the cold glass, she closed her eyes and tried to remember her *mamm's* smile. *Will I always remember her face so vividly? The smell of her favorite lotion and the softness of her touch? What her voice sounded like when she called my name?*

Opening her eyes, Emma felt fresh tears running down her face as she watched Nathan whisper something in her mother's ear. It had only been three months since she'd left Sugarcreek to come home to help care for her ailing *mamm*, but by the looks of things, Marie had found her own contentment with Nathan. The emptiness she felt in her Amish *mamm's* passing was, for a second at least, replaced with a genuine gladness of her English mother's happiness. Noticing Marie continued to wear her head-covering gave her hope that she had indeed found her way back to *Gott*.

Wiping a small opening on the fogged window, Emma realized they were about to pass the Yoder's Strawberry Acres sign. Within a few minutes, they would be pulling into her *datt's* driveway, where she would have to face the hundreds of people that would be waiting to pay their condolences. She was sure their neighbors meant well, but all she wanted to do was retreat to the privacy of her room. The next few hours would be harder on her than the last six months had been. Only her closest friends, Samuel and Katie Yoder, and her immediate family knew she wasn't really Emma Byler. But in all fairness, she didn't really care who knew. She still felt like Emma Byler, even if her birth certificate stated she was Elizabeth Cooper.

Not wanting to leave the warmth of the van, Emma stayed still as they pulled up to the front door. Waiting for the driver to get direction from Nathan, she looked over to the porch and instantly remembered one of the last good days Stella had. They sat on the porch enjoying a late warm spell as they drank a glass of her *mamm's* favorite mint tea. It was *Mamm* who had reminded her to stop trying to write her story. She told her only *Gott* knew what he had planned for any of them. Her job was to have enough faith that she would trust Him to write the next chapter, whatever that might be. At the time, little did she know the next chapter would be this.

Parking his truck, Daniel walked to the side of the van, opened the door and let Nathan out. Watching Nathan hold out his hand to help Marie from her seat, he smiled at the gentleness with which he treated his mother. Deciding to stay in Willow Springs when he brought Emma home, he hadn't witnessed how close they had become over the last few months. Even with the bleakness of the day, he smiled when he caught his mother's eye.

Marie looked toward the back seat. "Are you ready?" she asked Emma.

Nodding her head once and crawling around the middle seat, Emma pulled her bonnet tight to ward off the wind that swept around the van.

Letting Nathan guide their mother up the stairs, Daniel and Emma stopped when they saw Bishop Shetler standing near the front door. It was Daniel who reached up and pulled Marie's coat to get her attention. "What's he doing here?"

"Hush!" Marie said, turning her head back to him quickly. "He's Emma's grandfather, and I assume he's here for the same reason everyone else is. Please don't make a scene. Be cordial for Emma's sake, at least."

Walking up the stairs, Nathan stopped and shook the Bishop's hand before holding the door open for Emma and Marie. Without saying a word or making eye contact, Daniel took the door from Nathan and let him follow his mother and sister in the house.

A stern voice came behind him. "Daniel, can I have a word with you?"

"I think the time for a word or two has long passed," Daniel said, not missing a beat. "I don't have anything to say to you." As quickly as he opened the door he let it close, leaving his grandfather out in the cold.

Books by Tracy Fredrychowski

The Amish of Lawrence County Series
Secrets of Willow Springs - Book 1

Secrets of Willow Springs - Book 2

The Women of Lawrence County

Join the Amish Readers Club and get 10 recipes from the
Women of Lawrence County
https://tracyfredrychowski.com/sweettreat/

What did you think?

First of all, thank you for purchasing

Secrets of Willow Springs – Book 2.

I know you could have picked any number of books to read, but
you picked this book and for that I am extremely grateful. I hope it
added value and quality to your everyday life. If so, it would be
really nice if you could share this book with your friends and
family on Social Media.

If you enjoyed this book and found some benefit in reading it, I'd
like to hear from you and hope that you could take some time to
post a review on Amazon. Your feedback and support will help me
improve my writing craft for future projects.

Glossary of Pennsylvania Dutch "Deutsch" Words

Ausbund. Amish songbook.
boppli. Baby.
bruder. Brother
datt. Father or dad.
denki. "Thank You."
doddi. Grandfather.
doddi haus. A small house next to or attached to the main house.
fraa. Wife.
g'may. Community.
haus. House.
ja. "Yes."
kapp. Covering or prayer cap.
kinner. Children.
mamm. Mother or mom.
mei lieb. "My love."
mommi. Grandmother.
mun. Husband.
nee. "No."
Ordnung. Order or set of rules the Amish follow.
rumshpringa. "Running around" period.
schwester. Sister.
singeon. Singing/youth gathering.

The Amish are a religious group that is typically referred to as Pennsylvania Dutch, Pennsylvania Germans or Pennsylvania Deutsch. They are descendants of early German immigrants to Pennsylvania and their beliefs center around living a conservative lifestyle. They arrived between the late 1600s and the early 1800s to escape religious persecutions in Europe. They first settled in Pennsylvania with the promise of religious freedom by William Penn. Most Pennsylvania Dutch still speak a variation of their original German language as well as English.

Appendix

Emma's Apple Crisp

Ingredients:
6 large Granny Smith apples
1 cup quick oats
¾ cup brown sugar
½ cup flour
½ cup cold butter
2 tsp. cinnamon

Instructions:
Preheat oven to 350°
Peel and thinly slice apples and place in ungreased 9"x9" square baking dish.
Add remaining ingredients in a mixing bowl.
Using a pastry blender, cut cold butter into mixture until it resembles coarse crumbs.
Bake for 30 minutes.
OPTIONAL: Serve warm with vanilla ice cream and drizzle with caramel sauce.

Makes 9 servings

About the Author

Tracy Fredrychowski lives a life similar to the stories she writes. Striving to simplify her life, she often shares her simple living tips and ideas on her website and blog at tracyfredrychowski.com.

Growing up in rural northwestern Pennsylvania, country living was instilled in her from an early age. As a young woman, she was traumatized by the murder of a young Amish woman in her rural Pennsylvania community, and she became dedicated to sharing stories of their simple existence. She inspires her readers to live God-centered lives through faith, family, and community. If you would like to enjoy more of the Amish of Lawrence County, she invites you to join her in her Private Facebook Group. There she shares her friend Jim Fisher's Amish photography, recipes, short stories, and an inside look at her favorite Amish community nestled in northwestern Pennsylvania, deep in Amish Country.

Instagram - https://www.instagram.com/tracyfredrychowski/
Facebook - https://www.facebook.com/tracyfredrychowskiauthor
FB Group https://www.facebook.com/groups/tracyfredrychowski/